"Bring in the prisoners."

The doors at the back of the mess opened, and waiters wheeled two serving carts before the head table. A domed silver lid rested on each cart.

When the first cover was lifted the Great Leader smiled.

Only the shaved head of the prisoner was revealed. It was completely immobilized; a leather collar strapped the young Asian's neck to the table, and metal bands were clamped around his head.

The prisoner's face was white. His eyes were glistening pools of terror. The waiter slowly and carefully lifted away the top of the prisoner's shiny skull. The Great Leader stared hungrily at the quivering gray matter that lay exposed. He swallowed and then raised his arm as he cried, "To the eternal future of the Red Vengeance."

The Great Leader then reached forward and gouged a chunk of living brain from the prisoner's cranium with a silver spoon and brought it to his lips.

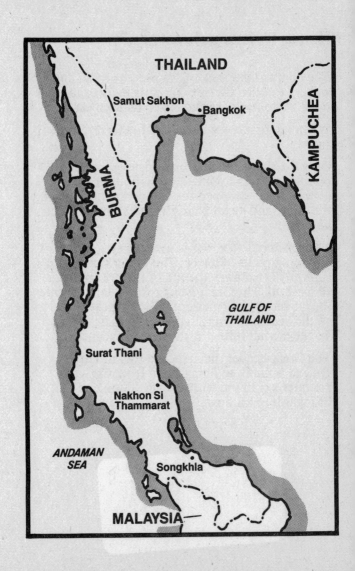

SOBs
SOLDIERS OF BARRABAS

RED VENGEANCE

JACK HILD

A GOLD EAGLE BOOK FROM
WORLDWIDE

TORONTO • NEW YORK • LONDON • PARIS
AMSTERDAM • STOCKHOLM • HAMBURG
ATHENS • MILAN • TOKYO • SYDNEY

First edition September 1986

ISBN 0-373-61614-7

Special thanks and acknowledgment to
Robin Hardy for his contributions to this work.

Printed in Canada

1

The warm water of the Gulf of Thailand heaved like half-set jelly in a giant's bowl. The water was fathomless, its black surface reflecting the pinpoint lights of the tiny stars overhead.

Alex Nanos whispered to the other men in the small rubber dinghy. "No moon." The wiry, muscular Greek dipped the aluminum oars quietly below the surface and pulled. "God's on our side tonight."

Half a klick across the gently rolling sea the darkened luxury liner *Empress Christina* floated in silence. A few lights burned dimly on the bridge. The portholes were dark.

"The goddess," Lee Hatton commented softly, almost under her breath. In response to Alex's quizzical look, she continued. "The moon is Diana, a goddess. Also the huntress. The warrior maiden." The M-16 resting in the dark-haired woman's hand paid silent homage.

Tonight Lee Hatton was also a huntress.

"Moon god come very soon." William Starfoot II—Billy Two to his friends—the full-blooded Osage from Oklahoma, had lapsed into a sullen, ruminative silence as time fired the tension in the air.

Lee Hatton and Alex Nanos nodded.

"Ten minutes," Nanos said, dipping the oars again and pulling the dinghy solidly forward under the cover of night. "Yup, just enough time to move in on the rats and wipe 'em out."

"Can it!" boomed a commanding voice from the other end of the little boat. "We're too close for chitchat now."

Nile Barrabas didn't turn when he spoke.

He wore a wet suit, and his face was smeared with black camouflage paint. His prematurely white hair, a souvenir of a Vietcong head wound, was covered by a tight-fitting hood. Like the others, he wore soft-soled landing boots. The belt around his waist was studded with grenades.

From the front of the dinghy he watched the dark ship loom larger. The other members of the American covert action team fell silently into their private thoughts.

A terror squad of Chinese, South Korean, Arab Black September and Japanese Red Army extremists had seized the luxury passenger liner a week earlier during its cruise from Australia to Hong Kong. They threatened to blow it up with all passengers aboard unless several hundred political prisoners in Seoul were released.

Most of the passengers were elderly Americans.

America was in a fighting, angry mood.

The President vowed that the United States would never be held hostage. The terrorists would be shown no quarter.

Barrabas and his soldiers got the call. The hijackers threatened to kill the first hostages at sunrise. Barrabas's instructions were simple: eliminate the terrorists before they got started.

Barrabas shifted his weight and checked out the MAG ejector straddling his chest for the last time. Three long, curving hooks tipped with barbs protruded from the wide barrel. Billy Two, sitting at the back of the IBS, held a second grappling device similar to Barrabas's.

As for the moon, Barrabas didn't give a damn whether it was god, goddess or green cheese. If they weren't in the right place before it rose, they were all going to be sitting ducks.

Dead ones.

He raised his image-intensification binoculars and scanned the deck of the darkened ship. He saw two men standing at the bow—small, dark shapes whose lighter colored shirts caught the little bit of available light. A third one left the bridge and descended to join his buddies.

"Let's go in halfway down the port side," Barrabas whispered to Nanos. "There are three of them at the bow, more on the bridge. They've staked out the stern. But the side's clear."

The hull of the giant ship rose above them like a smooth, steel precipice. The little rubber boat ascended the crest of a small wave and softly nudged the side of the ship. Barrabas checked his chronometer. Two minutes to go. He signaled Billy Two.

The two mercs raised the launchers and rested the long barrels across their shoulders. They aimed upward with an eighty-five-degree azimuth and waited. The last seconds before battle pass slowly. Then suddenly it's there.

ON THE OTHER SIDE OF THE SHIP a second inflatable boat closed in against the metal hull. Nate Beck carefully placed a steel magnet on the side of the ship and hooked a nylon cord through it to hold the little boat steady.

Claude Hayes, a big muscular black man and an expert scuba diver, swung his legs over the side.

"We're almost five minutes short," he whispered to Geoff Bishop, the other merc in the boat.

"We'll be okay," Bishop told him.

Nate Beck hoisted a MAG launcher into his arms and checked the three-pronged hook.

Hayes nodded. He pushed himself forward and slipped beneath the surface of the waves like a shadow dissolving in water.

The silent night was suddenly broken by an ominous sound—the distant drone of airplanes approaching from the west. Fast.

IN THE THAI PROVINCIAL CAPITAL of Songkhla, a coterie of Thai navy officers and one American naval officer stood anxiously around a radar console. The wide plate-glass windows looked out on the shimmering lights in the harbor, where hundreds of fishing boats floated at anchor. Beyond, the water of the Gulf of Thailand was a great black mass rimming the night. U.S. Navy Commander Lee Ryder sat at the console beside Captain Son Boka of the Royal Thai Navy. Both men anxiously watched the radar screen. A bright green dot marked the position of the *Empress Christina*. Five smaller blips appeared suddenly, traveling at great speed.

"Your air force is at 'er, Captain Boka!" Commander Ryder exclaimed. "Right on time!"

Boka turned to the radio operator sitting at a nearby station. "Make contact immediately," he ordered.

Overhead, the clock showed two minutes to midnight. Static burst from the speakers mounted above the consoles and was followed by sharp, angry jabbering in a foreign language.

"They hear the planes. They demand to know what is happening," the young sailor at the radio told Captain Boca and the American commander.

"Tell them the flyover is routine, to verify the safety of the American hostages," Boca instructed him. He looked at Commander Ryder for further instructions.

Ryder nodded. The American military man had passed the forty-eight-hour mark without sleep, yet the urgency of the situation, with hundreds of innocent lives at stake, kept him totally alert. Still, when he spoke next it was wearily. The words were those he never thought he would hear himself speak. His eyes met Captain Boca's. "Tell them we accede. Unconditionally. To all their demands."

THE FOUR MEN ON THE BRIDGE of the *Empress Christina* winced as the broad, flat undercarriages of the air force squadron soared past the windows.

"They are attacking, Ki Lim!" Mustafi Ali's hands went up as he involuntarily ducked, grabbing the checkered cotton kefireh, the traditional headgear of a renegade Arab terrorist, that he wore over his head. "Now is the time to..."

"Patience, Mustafi," the short, wiry Asian answered grimly. His voice barely concealed his own impatience with the combined assault force of terrorists who had seized the luxury liner.

"Now is the time for us to make good our escape!" Mustafi Ali's voice rose to an almost hysterical pitch. "You must get us out of here now!"

"You knew the chances of escape were only fifty-fifty," Ki Lim said sternly as he looked out of the bridge's windows.

The sound of the aircraft engines had faded. The returning calm seemed to reassure the Arab.

"But that is why we agreed to use your organization. And paid well for it, too."

Ki Lim turned finally to face Mustafi Ali. The Asian's dark eyes glinted like luminous beads in his bronzed, sea-roughened face. His long, thin mustache twitched with his mouth, which was almost always frozen in a snarl. He glanced coldly at the other two men standing on the bridge. The American captain of the *Empress Christina* was white, and large bags of darkened skin circled his eyes. The other man was Japanese, as short as Ki Lim, but lacking the Thai's weathered appearance. He held a large long-barreled handgun over his head, pressing the deadly end deep into the flesh of the American captain's neck.

A shrill, steady beep and a flashing red light on the instrument console signaled the reception of a radio message. Outside, the sound of aircraft engines again grew louder as the jets made a return run across the ship.

Mustafi Ali grabbed the microphone and shouted into it, swearing and cursing American imperialism. Ki Lim reached over and pushed a toggle on the console. The voice from the Thai naval station in Songkhla burst through a field of static on the bridge's loudspeakers. The final words of the shore message froze the terrorists. Mustafi Ali looked at Ki Lim, his eyes clouded with confusion and surprise.

"They have acceded to all our demands!" he said.

Ki Lim's dark eyes glinted like polished black stones. "It's too late now, though, isn't it?" The corners of his mouth twitched upward in a sardonic smile at the Arab's obvious discomfort. Mustafi Ali's face grew vacant with the realization of the truth of the Thai pirate's words.

The airplanes were almost overhead again, filling the bridge with the deafening noise of their powerful jet engines. Moving slowly and smoothly, Ki Lim turned toward the frightened captain, who towered more than a foot over the little Asian. He grabbed the American's hair with one hand, forcing him to his knees. With a simultaneous movement of his other arm, he took the gun from the Japanese guard.

The captain's words froze in his mouth. Ki Lim calmly pressed the barrel of the gun to the prisoner's temple and pulled the trigger.

The jet fighters directly overhead drowned the noise of the bullet. The captain's head exploded outward against the wall of the bridge in a huge splash of blood and gray matter, then the body slumped to the floor.

Ki Lim handed the gun back to the Japanese terrorist and turned back to the console.

"It is all your fault," Mustafi Ali shouted at Ki Lim. "You told me to give the order. I should never have listened. When we cannot give them the hostages, they will..."

"We still have this," the Thai pirate interrupted, patting a detonation box resting on the instrument console. A cord of wires thick as a man's wrist led to the floor and out one of the bridge's doors.

"This ship is, after all, a floating bomb. Let them come for us. They will be blown to smithereens."

NATE BECK RAISED THE LAUNCHER over his shoulder and aimed high up the side of the ship.

"Sure you're all right?" Bishop asked. Beck was known on the team for his expertise with computers and electronics. Unlike the others, he'd had little military experience when Barrabas had recruited him. When he had begun, he was, as Alex Nanos had once put it bluntly, a lousy shot.

"Sure, I'm sure," Beck answered confidently, flashing a smile. "I been practicing."

Bishop nodded. "Sorry."

"It's okay. They don't give us a second chance."

Bishop watched the second hand sweep around the luminous dial of his watch. "One minute," he told Beck. "Fifty seconds, forty..."

The drone of the engines grew louder as the squadron of fighters from the Royal Thai Air Force approached the *Empress Christina*. Almost as suddenly as the noise began, the airplanes' running lights appeared, throwing a colorful sheen on the rolling sea.

Nate shifted slightly and raised the launcher to its final position. "Fuck. What a noise," he muttered as the vibration pounded his ears.

"Ten seconds, five seconds!" Bishop shouted, counting down to the final pause.

The squadron was coming in low and fast over the water, barely above the level of the *Empress Christina*'s twin stacks. Two of the five warplanes broke formation and veered along the port side of the great ship while the other three angled starboard.

The second hand on Bishop's watch hit home.

"Do it!" he yelled.

Nate Beck squeezed the trigger on the launcher.

The long metal tube shuddered, the recoil pushing him back. The rocket-launched grappling hook flew high, spinning the long steel cord behind. The three-pronged hook curved gracefully and fell over the starboard railing. The clatter of metal hitting metal was drowned by the roar of the Thai fighters as they soared low and loud over the top of the ship.

Bishop stood, causing the little rubber dinghy to sink sharply into the water. He grabbed the steel cable and tugged. It held. He reached high and pulled himself up, swinging out of the dinghy and planting his feet against the hull. Below him, a light shone up from the water. A second later Claude Hayes's dark head surfaced.

The roar of the jet fighters had faded, but already it was growing again as they turned for the second flyover.

Hayes hurled a heavy object into the dinghy. "They had the stern wired to blow," he told the two men. "This ship is a bomb waiting to go off!"

Bishop cast one last look back, grimly meeting eyes with Hayes and Beck. "See you at the top," he said. With his boots scrambling on the metal hull of the hijacked ship, he pulled himself up.

BARRABAS SWUNG OVER the ship's railing on the other side of the *Empress Christina*. He pulled his Commando into firing line and glanced quickly at the grappling hook. The steel hooks were clawed tightly against the ship's railing. Billy Two's aim with the launcher had been good.

The narrow deck that ran along the first-floor staterooms was empty. He surveyed the deck above, where the *Empress Christina*'s lifeboats hung from their davits. Several of them glowed with a light sheen of highly polished fiberglass. They were the high-speed motor launches the terrorists had used to board.

The ship was silent. Almost too silent. Barrabas felt a sick chill in the pit of his stomach.

The steel cable jerked, and Lee Hatton swung over the side of the ship. Her nostrils flared, and she sniffed the air.

"Smell it?" Barrabas asked her. The question was rhetorical.

Lee nodded.

It was the smell of death. The rank odor of decaying bodies. There had already been killing here.

Alex Nanos's head appeared at the top of the rappel rope, and Barrabas quickly reached out to help him clamber over the edge. The rope jerked tightly as Billy Two began his ascent. The Greek's face wizened as he caught the smell. "Bastards have already started their slaughter," he muttered, patting the barrel of his autorifle. "Now it's our turn."

Soon Billy Two stood on deck with the other three mercs. Barrabas nodded curtly, and Billy Two and Nanos turned in the direction of the stern. Barrabas and Hatton raced for the bow.

The former U.S. Army colonel glanced at the luminous dial of his chronometer. The second hand closed in on five minutes after midnight. A soft glow on the far horizon heralded the rising full moon. Right on time. Suddenly the rapid chatter of autofire cut the night.

The battle had begun.

GEOFF BISHOP CROUCHED SILENTLY on the deck of the liner as Nate Beck reached the top of the rappel rope.

The same rank odor of decaying flesh Barrabas had encountered on the other side of the ship floated heavily in the still air. Nate's face twisted against the putrid smell. He felt his stomach climb into his throat.

"Dead bodies," Bishop muttered softly. "They've been killing."

Beck stood on the deck of the liner. He swallowed to fight off the nausea. "How much time?" he asked.

"Less than a minute." Already a low, luminous glow from the edge of the rising moon spread over the water. The rope strained against the grappling hooks with Claude Hayes's weight, and soon the black man's head rose over the side of the ship.

"Get down!" Bishop said urgently. He reached out a hand for Claude Hayes.

Beck crouched in the shadows. He could feel his stomach heaving against the smell of decomposition and tightened his throat against it. The second hand on his chronometer swept around. Zero hour and seven. Moonrise. He fought his rising stomach.

"Shit, man, it stinks," Hayes muttered as he hoisted one leg over the railing.

"Shhh," Bishop hissed. Hayes followed his eyes.

At the bow of the ship a man was walking down the starboard deck in their direction. The moon's first luminosity glowed on his light-colored shirt. He carried a rifle loosely across his chest.

Nate gagged. He pressed his hands against his mouth to stifle it, but his natural repulsion to the stench of death took over.

Bishop let go of Hayes and pulled his rifle up just as the terrorist swung in their direction.

Orange muzzle flash lit the deck, and the mercs felt the autofire wing past. A bullet ricocheted off steel. Hayes grunted with pain. His left hand flew from the ship's railing. Blood splashed through the air, and the black man fell backward toward the water.

BARRABAS JERKED HIS HEAD at Billy Two and Nanos, signaling them toward the stern. He ran forward to the bridge with Lee Hatton. The plan was to board in two parties on opposite sides. Nanos and Starfoot were to join up with Claude Hayes at the stern. Hatton, Bishop and Beck were to clean off the bow while Barrabas went for the bridge.

That was the plan. But it sounded as if Bishop and the others were in serious difficulty.

The moon was half over the horizon, and a wide silver river ran across the Gulf of Thailand; the ship was illuminated in its eerie secondhand light. Shouts echoed across the front of the ship, accompanied by more autofire from farther down the starboard side.

Two men, black mummies in the half-light, burst around the corner of the front deck. Lee Hatton slid to her knees, squeezing the trigger to full auto.

Barrabas kept running. The stairs to the bridge were only a few meters away. Bullets pinged on the metal wall. He tugged a grenade from his belt and bit the end like the rind of an orange.

Hatton's auto chatter put them on hold.

One took a head shot smack on. His face blew open from his nose outward. The other ducked back behind the corner.

Where there was one, there were probably more coming. Barrabas pulled the pin with his teeth and counted the three more steps it took to reach the stairs. At the last minute he ran wide and threw a long curve. Someone around the corner shouted. Barrabas ducked into the stairwell.

The shout died in the blast and was never heard again.

Instead, the night was rent by the explosion and pounding autofire.

The fireworks had begun.

2

On the deck at the stern of the *Empress Christina*, Farouk al Nah and Tanka Soji listened to padded feet running down the port side. They pressed tightly into the wall and waited for the moment to rush into the open and mow the attackers down.

Both terrorists were tensed to kill. Their leader, Mustafi Ali, had been right. The imperialists would never give in. They would attempt to storm the ship. But Farouk al Nah and his Japanese Red Army cohort were prepared to die as one. All the men knew the ship was set to blow up. That did not prevent them from personally depriving some of the attackers of their lives.

Farouk wanted to see the devil dog American's eyes when he sent him to Satan. He made sure his Japanese brother Tanka Soji was second in line.

Alex Nanos and Billy Two pounded toward the stern. The Greek took a lead on the Osage, leveling his Colt Commando and driving against the wall as he swung around the corner.

Farouk al Nah and Tanka Soji heard the footsteps reach the corner.

"Now!" Farouk shouted.

He twisted into the open and slammed full force into Alex Nanos. The collision locked both men together, pinning their rifles between them. Nanos snarled. Al Nah saw the devil dog's eyes, and terror pierced the terrorist's soul. The Greek jerked his left arm forward, swinging the butt of his rifle between Farouk's legs.

"Nyaaaaaa!" al Nah shrieked, driving the air from his lungs. He fell back, giving Nanos room to maneuver. Tanka Soji came to his buddy's rescue with a bloodcurdling death scream. The full moonlight glinted off the terrorist's teeth. He raised his rifle and aimed at Nanos.

Billy Two barreled around the corner.

"Alex, you're full of spitfire," he muttered, reaching his long, thick arms for Soji, "and then you get us in shit." Billy Two wrapped his ten-inch hand around the top of Soji's head. The Red Army terrorist felt himself leaving the ground as the giant took hold of his neck with the other hand.

Nanos swatted Farouk al Nah across the face with the barrel of his rifle, stunning him. Then he grabbed the terrorist at crotch and collar, threw his strength into his upper torso and swung. Al Nah spun like a runaway flywheel through the air and over the side of the ship.

Billy Two raised the second killer off the deck and twisted head and body in opposite directions. The sickening crunch of neck vertebrae signaled the end of Farouk. Billy Two dropped the limp body and glared at Alex.

"No more smartass, Alex," he said, as if it were an apology.

Nanos nodded his head, speechless. "Okay, Billy. You lead."

A volley of autofire sounded from the starboard side. A line of enemy riflemen, their backs to Nanos and Billy Two, blasted bullets down the ship, ducking behind a bulkhead when return fire answered. More terrorists were shouting on the upper deck.

Billy Two put his hand in front of Nanos to stop him. He signaled with a finger to his lips, then motioned to the bulkhead and the deck above.

The two mercs slipped grenades from their belts. They pulled the pins, looked at each other and counted down. One thousand, two thousand, three thousand, four...

Nanos looked at his grenade. Then he looked at Billy Two's. Four and a half.

"Hey, boys!" Nanos grinned and shouted. He tossed his grenade into the air, and it arced onto the deck above. Billy Two lobbed an easy underhand over the bulkhead. They threw themselves flat on the deck as the concussion waves blew over them.

STILL GAGGING FROM HIS NAUSEA, Nate Beck swiveled his Colt Commando and pulled the trigger.

The short three-round burst punched into the terrorist, shoving him backward. He fell with his arms and legs in the air. Bishop lunged as Hayes tipped backward off the ship. The black man grabbed the rappel rope with his right hand, breaking his fall. Nate jumped up to pull Hayes over the side.

"There'll be more," Bishop whispered quickly as he and Beck strained at Hayes's weight. Hayes's left hand was red with blood.

Shrill shouts came from the bridge, and doors were flung open as the enemy force ran to repel the SOBs' attack. More autofire and an explosion came from the port side opposite them. Barrabas had landed.

Bishop felt a ricocheting metal sting on the side of his face. As he scanned the decks, multiple muzzle flashes burst from the stern. A narrow alcove afforded eighteen inches of cover, and the three warriors darted inside it just as another terrorist appeared on the bow.

Bullets zinged past. The man at the bow fell, hit by one of his own men firing from the stern. Nate Beck dropped to his knees and blew his rounds off on full auto. The defenders at the stern jumped out of sight behind a bulkhead. One didn't make it; he rolled through the railing, disappearing forever in the watery depths of the Gulf. Nate pressed back against the ship's wall as more bullets flew past his face.

Hayes ripped open his wet suit and, with his one good hand, tore a strip from the front of his T-shirt. Bishop took it and wrapped it around Hayes's other hand. The bullet had hit between the thumb and the index finger, tearing out a lump of flesh.

"Shit, man. That hurts so bad!" Claude's face twisted with pain. "What happened to you?"

Bishop wiped his hand across his jaw. It came away with blood on it. "Nothing serious," Bishop told him, tying the bandage into a knot. "Just stay low. Nate and I will take care of this."

"Hell, no. I got one good hand left, and it's real trigger-happy."

Autofire sailed past them from both directions, pinning them against the wall. Bishop slipped two grenades from his belt and handed one to Hayes.

"Can you throw this?"

Hayes bared his teeth in a great smile. "Is the Pope Catholic?"

They pulled the pins.

On the count of two, they were interrupted by a double explosion on the stern. They heard a victory screech, followed by a chilling war whoop.

Nanos and Billy Two were coming around the corner, autorifles blasting. Hayes looked at his grenade. It seemed as if it was no longer needed. He tossed it over the side of the ship just as Bishop threw his toward the bow.

Billy Two and Nanos slammed to a halt beside the other three mercs.

"How ya doing, boys!" Nanos shouted, his eyes mad with excitement. "Pinned down? We cleaned out the stern!"

The two mercs kept going, tossing off quick three-round bursts toward the bow as further disincentive. Autofire echoed from the other side of the ship.

Hayes cradled the butt of his rifle along his right arm and wedged it between his elbow and his chest. "Come on!" he shouted to Bishop and Nanos. "Let's take the bridge!"

KI LIM EYED MUSTAFI ALI. The terrorist leader began to tremble when the din of autofire and grenade explosions split the silence.

"It was a ruse!" the terrorist shouted. "They tricked us!"

He clutched the console and looked out over the bow of the ship just in time to see the brief yellow flash of an explosion eliminate three of his men. Two more explosions rocked the ship from the stern. "We'll kill them. Praise Allah, we'll kill them all!"

Ki Lim reached toward the detonator box and pulled the toggle. The digital clock face spun to show five minutes, and the seconds were ticking down. From his position near the window, he looked down at the stairs leading to the lower deck.

One of the attackers, a man dressed in black and moving very quickly, was ascending the steps, holding his autorifle as if he intended to use it.

Ki Lim watched for a few brief seconds, fascinated by this formidable opponent. Halfway up the steps, the attacker pulled the hood back from his head and looked up. Ki Lim's eyes met his. The image of nearly white hair and stark blue eyes imprinted on his memory like a photograph.

Just then, Mustafi Ali shouted an order at the other terrorist on the bridge. Ki Lim stepped over the body of the dead captain and backed toward a door that led into the ship's staterooms. Quietly he stepped through, closing it tightly behind him. Then he ran through the dimly lit corridor, holding his breath against the thick stench of decay.

"Order the others to retreat to the bridge!" Ali shouted at the Japanese Red Army compatriot. "We will escape with the motor launches! Ki Lim!"

He looked around for the pirate guide, his alarm turning to blind fury when he saw bloody footprints leading to the cabin door. He would kill the coward for this.

The Red Army terrorist opened the door to the bridge deck, and suddenly his body buckled backwards. Red flowers bloomed across his back, and the 7.76 Commando bullets kept going, blasting fist-sized holes in the man's chest as they tumbled out.

Mustafi Ali looked at the detonator. It turned to three minutes and kept counting. He looked up and saw the face of a white-haired devil.

Barrabas towered over the body of the dead Red Army man, his eyes burning. He held the door open with one hand, steadying his autorifle against his hip with the other.

Mustafi gasped. "H-h-he escapes!" The Arab terrorist pointed to the door through which Ki Lim had just vanished.

"You the leader?" Barrabas snarled.

Ali raised his hands and nodded.

"Where are the hostages?"

"All dead!" Ali sounded as if he was sorry. He should have been.

Barrabas didn't even hesitate as he squeezed the trigger.

Mustafi Ali knew exactly what hit him, times three, right in the face. He just didn't have time to think about it before he splattered to the floor, his brains dribbling through the cracks in his shattered skull.

"Colonel!" Nate Beck shouted as he arrived on the bridge.

Scattered reports of autofire echoed from around the ship as the other mercs took care of the remaining opposition. Barrabas pointed to the detonator on the navigation console, and he and Beck watched as the seconds spun down to two minutes and kept going.

"Can you defuse that?" Barrabas asked.

The computer expert examined the wires as Barrabas stepped across the bodies and tried the door that led into the ship's interior. It was locked. He aimed his rifle and pounded three bullets into it, then kicked it open.

Bloody footprints led down a long corridor. He remembered the motor launches suspended from the lifeboat davits on the port side near the stern and knew there was a faster way to get there. He jumped back into the bridge just as Lee Hatton arrived, her face white and tense.

"I found the hostages, Colonel. Slaughtered like cattle. They turned the ship's ballroom into a bloodbath with an M-60."

"I figured. Let's get moving. One of these bastards is getting away."

They ran through the door and down the upper deck on the port side. Ahead of them in the moonlight the hydraulic arms of the lifeboat davits stretched over the water, spinning out their steel cables. Barrabas could make out the dark shape of a man at the steering wheel of the high-speed motor launch halfway down the side of the ship.

The colonel brought his autorifle up and fired off a three-round burst. The man in the boat turned to look up at the ship. Orange muzzle explosions flashed, and the two mercs jumped back against the side of the upper deck.

"Bastard!" Barrabas swore. He squeezed full auto and ran forward just as the fiberglass hull of the motor launch slapped against the surface of the water. The motor roared into life, and the boat moved quickly across the water. Barrabas's bullets drove into the sea as the launch swiftly drew out of range.

"Come on!" he snapped at Hatton, turning back to the bridge.

From the deck below they heard a scream followed by a short burst of autofire. Two of the terrorists dived headfirst off the side of the ship. Lee Hatton leaned her autorifle over the railing, teeth clenched, and blew off the rest of her mag. The descending bodies twitched and jerked in midair, dead before they hit the water.

Nanos and Billy Two ran into the open on the bow and waved up at the woman warrior.

"Thanks, babe!" Alex cried.

Lee rolled her eyes.

"Babes don't kill," she shouted back. "I do."

Barrabas arrived at the bridge just as Hayes and Bishop stormed up the steps from the other side and crowded in. Nate Beck was leaning over the detonator. The metal cover was off, and his hands feverishly probed the electronic innards. The digital readout flashed to a minute and started counting down the seconds.

"There's no way, Colonel," Beck said without looking up. "I can defuse it, but not in fifty-four seconds."

"Then we bail out and swim for it!" Barrabas shouted. " Let's go! There's no time!"

The mercs fled the bridge and raced for the lower deck, running into Nanos and Billy Two on their way up. Barrabas checked his watch. Thirty seconds. Half a klick off the port bow, the inflatable seven-man dingy floated at sea.

"Buddy up and stay together when you hit the water!" Barrabas ordered.

Lee Hatton and Jeff Bishop were first at the side of the ship, dropping their mag belts and throwing their rifles aside. Without a second's hesitation, they climbed over the rail, stretched their arms and took perfectly poised dives off the ship.

Billy Two and Claude Hayes were next over. Nanos and Beck looked down the steep side and at each other.

"Don't look," Beck said.

"Headfirst!" Barrabas shouted, "or you won't make it."

Beck stretched out his arms, closed his eyes and fell forward.

Nanos gulped. "Sheeit!"

"Don't think about it," Barrabas told him, dropping his remaining grenades and spare mags as he scrambled over the railing. Fifteen seconds. "Jump, Alex."

The Greek leaped over the railing, letting go and kicking off. It was a long way down. When Nanos hit the air, Barrabas followed. He cut the water like the blade of a knife, going in deep. He scooped his arms forward to stop the descent into the depths and kicked upward. His last gulp of air seared at his lungs as he pulled his arms back and broke the surface.

Around him he counted off five heads bobbing to the surface of the moonlit sea. The mercs' powerful arms reached forward, pulling them away from the deadly ship.

"I can't find Claude!" Billy Two shouted with alarm, half a dozen meters away.

Just then the black man's head broke the surface of the water between the two men. He gulped desperately for air and held one arm in the air. For the first time Barrabas saw the blood-darkened bandage around Hayes's hand.

Barrabas and Billy Two swam toward Hayes with powerful strokes.

"Little trouble with my hand," Hayes muttered, still gasping for air.

"Grab his belt," Barrabas ordered, "and kick like hell."

Barrabas glanced at his chronometer. Three seconds. Two. The three mercs moved away from the shadow of the *Empress Christina*.

Then the ship blew.

A deafening explosion sounded from the stern of the ship, throwing a sudden orange glow momentarily around the three swimmers. There was a slight pause, then a crescendo of sound as the terrorist explosives blew, working their way up the ship toward the bow.

Suddenly the night flashed bright yellow, and the concussion waves from a massive detonation battered the mercs. The sea heaved, and the midsection of the *Empress Christina* blew high into the air as a raging fireball glistened like blood across the roughened waves.

3

The hot sun pressed through the louvered shutters, casting lines of light and shadow across the floor and along the naked man lying on the narrow, rumpled bed. The air in the little hotel room was thick with heat, the smells of stale cooking and old cigar smoke. The morning din of the street outside—crying children, merchants hawking theirs wares, animals awaiting selection and slaughter—was unmerciful.

Nile Barrabas pressed his eyelids shut against the prying fingers of sunlight. A big, heavy bowling ball rolled back and forth inside his skull. He winced as it crashed against one side, then rolled and pounded to the other. He flapjacked onto his stomach and pulled the pillow over his head to drown the noise.

It didn't work.

Finally he stretched out one arm, hitting the little bedside table, and felt blindly with his hand until it struck glass. The bottle. It tipped and clattered forward before he could close his hand around it. His arm swooped down, and he grabbed it by the neck as it fell. It was the empty one, and he let go. It hit the wooden floor and rolled away. He moved his hand to the top of the table until he came to the other bottle. It didn't tip. It was still half-full.

Breakfast. He threw the pillow aside, turned his head and pulled the bottle to his lips. The warm Scotch felt good, burning his throat on the way down. The bowling ball felt more like a tennis ball now.

He opened his eyes.

The paint scaled off the ceiling like skin on a leper. For a brief second he wondered where he was. A bad sign. Then he remembered. Songkhla, the provincial Thai capital, a fishing city on the Gulf of Thailand. A chunk of paint left the ceiling and fluttered slowly down, landing on his cheek. It tickled. He reached up and brushed it off, then knocked back the rest of the Scotch.

Much better. A little wasted, but better. He sat up and swung his legs off the side of the bed. The wallpaper was soiled with great yellow rings of condensation, the little sink was brown, the curtains at the shuttered windows were barely more than rags and the door was scarred by screw holes and splintered wood where countless locks had been broken off and replaced. There was no toilet, but a cracked and stained bidet sat by the sink. He walked over and used it. By the time he returned to the bed, his head was swimming again.

He tugged on a cord hanging from the ceiling, and somewhere far off he heard little bells tingle. It was a first-class hotel. It had room service. For the first time he noticed that the skin over his left bicep stung. He screwed up his face. He didn't remember being wounded there, but a vague memory clawed at him of something he had done the night before. He had the desperate feeling that he didn't want to remember. He skipped it and went back to the beginning. There had to be some reason why he had ended up with a hangover in a stinking fleabag hotel in Thailand.

He'd been given the job of eliminating a group of terrorists holding hostages on an ocean liner. Now both terrorists and hostages were dead—and at least one of the murderers had got away.

The SOBs had tasted defeat.

The mercs had been left swimming in the Gulf of Thailand as the charred and twisted wreckage of the *Empress Christina* had burned around them. Thai navy helicopters had plucked them from the little IBS and had returned them to the naval base at Songkhla.

Barrabas had gone out to celebrate by drinking himself blind. That part he remembered. There were other things best forgotten, like the stinging skin on his left arm.

A knock on the door saved him.

A small, thin Thai opened the door. He had a big smile and carried a tray of steaming, unrecognizable food. Four little girls peered out from around his legs, staring wide-eyed and curious at the big, muscled American sitting naked on the bed. Barrabas reached for the sheet and pulled it across his lap. The little girls giggled again, pressing their hands over their mouths.

"American sir feel better now? American sir eat?" The man bowed his head deferentially to punctuate each sentence.

The little girls giggled louder and chattered to one another. They were pointing to his shoulder. Barrabas looked down.

"Oh, jeez," he muttered. The tattoo spread across most of his bicep. The colors were bright from the freshly injected ink, and the skin around it glowed pink from the irritation. He had to admit it was a lovely tattoo—some strange Indo-Chinese war god with four arms. Two held swords; the other two held severed heads.

"You make last night!" the little Thai said, beaming. "Is very nice!"

Barrabas nodded slowly. "Whatever you say." He knew from the first sip of Scotch that he was going to remember something awful about the night before. A tattoo. It made him feel like a cliché.

"My wife do!" the little Thai said proudly.

Barrabas remembered walking through the teeming crowds in Songkhla's red-light district along the harbor. The Thai's wife had obviously known a mark when she'd seen one coming. He'd thought she was offering something else when she'd winked and motioned with her head for him to come inside the little hotel.

Time to forget again.

"No food." Barrabas lifted the empty Scotch bottle with its neck suspended between his thumb and index finger and swung it back and forth. "One of these."

"No eat?" The hotelkeeper looked crestfallen at the tray he carried. "My wife make! Is very good!"

Barrabas just swung the bottle. The little girls let out another chorus of giggles. The Thai stuck his head outside the room and shouted, and a small, slender woman appeared. He handed her the tray, and she smiled shyly at Barrabas and handed her husband a bottle of Scotch.

He shooed the little girls away from his legs, entered the room and closed the door behind him. After he set the Scotch on the table, he sat on the bed beside Barrabas. His legs didn't reach the floor.

Barrabas ignored him and reached for the bottle.

"I don't remember inviting you to come in," he said slowly. He sucked back a long, sweet mouthful.

"American sir very drunk when he come last night," the Thai said.

"Is that how I got this?" He pointed to the tattoo. The Thai looked embarrassed.

"Is very nice. My wife do!"

"So you said."

"Is very powerful. To protect from evil eye. Is good luck. You very smart man."

Barrabas eyed him dubiously and swallowed another long gulp of Scotch. Finally he saw his clothes. They had been pressed, and now they lay neatly folded on a chair by the wall. He reached for them, throwing aside the pants and shirt. His Browning Hi-Power was on the bottom. He eyed the hotel owner warily as he picked it up and pulled the magazine. It was still loaded.

"What's the name of your hotel?" Barrabas asked.

The little Thai's eyes lit up with pride. "Golden Paradise. We are Golden Paradise. An honest business."

"Great. I'll recommend it to my friends."

The Thai looked earnestly at Barrabas, trying to wrap his lips around unfamiliar English words. "We aim . . . to please," he replied.

Barrabas just looked at him and slapped the magazine back inside the Browning Hi-Power. As he grabbed the bottle of Scotch again, the Thai proprietor bounced slightly on the bed. "Man come for you," he said.

Barrabas looked at the Thai.

"I tell him you sleep. No disturb."

"Good."

"He wait."

"Is there a back way out?" Barrabas asked, grabbing his pants.

"He very nice man," the Thai continued. "He say let you sleep. He U.S. Navy man. Wear hat." The hotel owner made the outline of a naval officer's peaked cap with his finger.

Barrabas slowed down as he buttoned up his shirt. It wasn't one of the mercs. It must be Commander Lee Ryder, the naval attaché who had acted as the SOBs' liaison with the Thai military authorities.

"He's still there?" Barrabas asked, tucking his shirt in.

"Yes. He wait. Very patient. I know U.S. Navy. I speak American. You go back to America, maybe you take me?"

Barrabas rolled up the long sleeves until they tightened around his biceps. The legs of the Indo-Chinese war god stuck out. He unrolled the sleeve enough to cover it.

The little Thai hotel owner looked disappointed.

"Secret," Barrabas explained, winking conspiratorially.

The Thai winked back, his look serious.

The big American reached into his pocket and pulled out a wad of U.S. dollars. A very honest house, the Golden Paradise. He rolled off five C-notes and thrust them into the hotelkeeper's hand.

"Buy yourself a ticket," he told him.

The Thai was stunned. Barrabas took another swig of whisky before heading for the door.

Commander Ryder paced the street in front of the Golden Paradise. "Look hard for me?" Barrabas called to him as he came out the front door.

Ryder was startled. The tall, lean American naval officer swung about to face him. "You look none the worse for wear," he said.

"You seem surprised."

Ryder laughed. "I followed the trail of the big white-haired American through half the taverns along the harbor until it led here. And from what I was told I figured you'd have a hell of a hangover today."

"Who are you talking about?"

"No one I know." Ryder laughed again. "Buy you a drink?"

"How about a real breakfast instead."

"Sure. I know a place that serves bacon and eggs American style. Then I'll take you for a drive. I've got something to show you."

SONGKHLA WAS ONE of Thailand's largest fishing ports, situated on the Malay Peninsula eighty kilometers from the Malaysian border. Its harbor was filled with hundreds of fishing trawlers, many of them painted bright, garish colors. The center of the old city was dominated by an ancient stone-walled fortress, with old iron cannon still projecting from the abutments.

"It was built hundreds of years ago to protect the Chinese pirates that controlled the Gulf of Thailand," Ryder explained to Barrabas as the two men drove out of the city an hour later. Beyond the harbor, the quiet turquoise waters of the Gulf lapped miles of white sand beaches. Shady groves of pine and casuarina trees lined the highway. The beaches were dotted with the rotting wooden skeletons of old boats.

"The Vietnamese boat people," Ryder continued, "float up on the beaches here. Thousands each month. Their boats are falling to pieces, and the people are usually more dead than alive."

"Then what happens to them."

"They end up in a holding center—more like a prison really—upcountry at Sikhiu. And there they wait, sometimes for years, for some western country to accept them."

The coastal plains of green rice paddies stretched to palm-covered inland mountains. Ten kilometers out of the city Ryder turned onto a thin gravel road leading to a small gathering of thatched huts surrounded by a wire fence. He drove through the gate, flashing his military identification to the unarmed Thai soldier who stood guard.

There were perhaps thirty of the low-roofed buildings, long and narrow like army barracks. Narrow packed-earth streets separated them into rows. Scantily clad children played with sticks and little cloth dolls, while women chatted, washed clothes at a tin-covered ablution house or cooked over little iron habachis. Men sat on the porches, not doing much of anything. One thing stood out for Barrabas—the vacant, frightened faces. Most of the Vietnamese people there looked as if they were in a state of semishock. He had seen it all before, years ago, as a soldier in Vietnam.

Ryder pulled up in front of a building with a big red cross over the door. Asian and Western nurses in starched white uniforms moved among the rows of beds inside, tending patients. As Barrabas and Ryder left the car, a buxom dark-haired woman left the infirmary and greeted them.

"Hi, Lee." She turned to Barrabas and said, "I'm Frances McGrattan. Everyone calls me Frankie, though." Then she looked back at Ryder. "Is this the American colonel you told me about?"

Ryder nodded.

"Well, Colonel Barrabas, I sure hope you can help us with our problem," Frankie said to the white-haired merc.

Barrabas gave Ryder a questioning look.

"Are you ready?" Ryder asked Frankie.

The nurse nodded. "I have two young girls who will talk. They're in the reception center."

The two men followed Frankie as she led them through the camp.

"Has Commander Ryder told you what these people are up against?" Frankie McGrattan asked Barrabas as they walked.

Barrabas shook his head. "Not a word."

"These people are leaving Vietnam by the thousands," Frankie began. "They buy passage with gold on boats that leave secretly at night. Of course, the brokers who arrange it all assure the people that they'll be safe. So a lot of parents send their teenage children, hoping they'll find a better life in another country—maybe even in America. The brokers will have a navigator on board to get them down the rivers and past the Vietnamese gunboats to the sea. Then another boat comes alongside and takes the navigator off. The people—and usually the boats are overcrowded—discover that they have no skilled sailors on board, little food and water, and on top of that, the boats are old and rotting, hardly suitable for a long-distance sea voyage. But that's not the worst of it."

Ryder spoke up. "Almost every boat that arrives on this coast has been attacked by pirates."

"Pirates!" Barrabas exclaimed. "In this day and age?"

Ryder nodded. "There have always been pirates in these waters. But in the last few years the numbers have increased dramatically. It started in the early seventies with the collapse of the fishing industry in the Gulf. It was an ecological disaster. The fish just disappeared. A lot of fishermen were left with expensive modern trawlers on their hands, so they started fishing for something else instead—small private yachts and cargo ships sailing these waters."

"But the boom really started with the exodus from Vietnam," Frankie picked up. "The refugees were easy pickings. They were completely undefended, and many of them carry valuable gold and jewelry. But even that's not the worst of it."

They stopped outside a small cinder block building with a United Nations flag drooping on a short flagpole outside. Nurse McGrattan led them inside, where two young Vietnamese girls in their midteens waited at a table.

"This is Duon Thi An and Kim Thi Linh," Frankie said.

The two girls looked up shyly at the two American men, then glanced away.

"They were found by the police on a beach near the Malaysian border a week ago and brought here for medical treatment. They're lucky to be alive. Can you speak Vietnamese, Colonel?"

Barrabas nodded. "I did in Vietnam. I haven't used it for a few years, though."

"If you run into trouble, I'll translate," Frankie offered. "I want you to listen to their story."

With an innocence beyond words, which reminded Barrabas of the young girls he had met years ago in the small villages and hamlets of Vietnam, the two teenagers began to talk.

Their parents had bought them passage out of Vietnam for four ounces of gold. Despite the broker's assurances, the two girls found themselves, along with forty-five others, on a leaky boat with no experienced sailors. Almost immediately they ran into a storm, which almost destroyed the boat.

"We prayed to the spirits of our ancestors," Linh said quietly. "And they watched over us."

By daybreak they drifted into the Gulf. The sea was calm. Now there was no wind for the sails. The sun was hot. They drifted for two days until they were almost out of food and water. When the sun rose on the third day, the little boat was surrounded by five huge fishing trawlers. The fishermen boarded and attacked them with lead pipes, knives and hammers.

Their possessions were torn to pieces as the pirates looked for gold. Anyone who resisted was savagely beaten. When they had finished, they seized five young women and took them aboard their ships.

Little Duon Thi An trembled, her voice barely audible, and tears welled in her eyes. "They kept us for ten days. And they raped us. Many, many times."

Kim Ti Linh spoke slowly, her voice hesitating over the words. "We wanted to die. But a child should not die before her parents, and our parents were alive in Vietnam. The pirates never spoke to us, and we didn't know what they were going to do."

On the tenth day the pirates separated the girls and transferred them to two other trawlers. For another three days they were raped repeatedly. Duon Thi An became physically ill, unable to eat, drink or sleep. She cried without stopping until finally the pirates put her back on the boat with Linh.

For seven more days the teenage girls endured sexual degradation until at last the pirates were finished with them. One night they were thrown overboard with only a plastic fuel container to keep them afloat.

"We couldn't swim," Linh told them. "And it was so scary because the big waves fell over us, making us choke. But we flapped our arms around and kicked our feet as we held on to the container. In the morning we saw boats in the distance, but they were too far to hear our calls for help."

For fifteen hours the two young girls drifted at sea. Finally, in the afternoon, some friendly fishermen found them. They gave the girls food and medicine, and a week later deposited them on the beach near Songkhla.

When An and Linh finished their story, Frankie McGrattan pounded the table with her fist. "If I ever get hold of those bastards, I'll cut their fucking balls off," she said with uncharacteristic ruthlessness. "And there are hundreds of stories like the one you just heard."

"None of the others who were aboard the boat that left Vietnam are known to have survived," Ryder said quietly. "A hundred and seventy-three boats reached Thailand last year. Of them, ninety-eight had been attacked at least twice. One boat was attacked eighteen times. Of twenty-five women on board, twenty-three were raped."

Barrabas looked at An and Linh, pained at the terrible agony they had endured and moved by their courage to survive. He took each one by the hand, squeezing tightly, and thanked them for their story.

"And thanks for listening," Frankie said. She led the two girls outside.

Barrabas and Ryder walked to the car. "You didn't bring me out here just to tug on my heartstrings," Barrabas said.

Ryder was evasive. "As I said earlier, the boat people aren't the only victims. The pirates also attack private yachts and cargo ships. They use modern trawlers with sophisticated radar and sonar equipment and deal in drugs, electronics smuggling and possibly the slave trade."

Barrabas looked at Ryder with raised eyebrows.

"Hundreds of Vietnamese women from the boats are still missing. Maybe they're dead, maybe...well, you heard."

"What are the authorities doing about it?

"They're trying, but they aren't accomplishing much. Thailand isn't a rich country. The antipiracy program has three small patrol boats and two unarmed propeller-driven aircraft that lack night capability.

"The pirates are controlled by various regional crime syndicates. They bribe local officials, extort protection money from fishermen and in some areas virtually control trading along the coast. The most powerful is a Chinese secret society called the Red Vengeance. The name first popped up more than a hundred years ago in the Opium Wars, and apparently it's still active.

"It's like the Mafia or Cosa Nostra. They ensure their members' loyalty with secret rituals, apparently things so horrible that to take part in them is to go beyond the limits of all human decency. And once done, you no longer are a part of any human society or social organization. You belong only to Red Vengeance, the brotherhood whose bonds are formed by these unspeakable acts."

Barrabas listened silently to Ryder. The two American military men reached the car and climbed in.

"I'm still waiting," Barrabas said finally.

Ryder looked at him.

"For the reason for bringing me to see all this."
Barrabas waved his hand toward the refugee camp as
the car pulled out of the gates.

Ryder seemed reluctant to continue. He drove for
a while before speaking. "Last night you said someone escaped from the ship before it blew."

Barrabas nodded. "When we boarded, I saw three
motor launches the terrorists had used to board the
ship. On the bridge I saw someone run through the
door that led into the ship. There was a bit of action
that delayed me. By the time I got around to the port
side, one of the launches was in the water and got
away."

Ryder nodded. "I had some interesting intelligence information early this morning from some
fishermen whose home port is in the Peril Islands—
an area off the coast reputed to be heavily infested
with pirates. They told me that the Red Vengeance
put those terrorists aboard the ship. And they were
paid a large amount of money and matériel for it. If
someone escaped, he had to be either Red Vengeance, or else one of their agents."

"You want me to check it out?" Barrabas asked.

Ryder shrugged and looked sideways at Barrabas.
"It would be unofficial. Your mandate ended when
the ship blew. But there's a group of progressive naval officers, some of them very high up, who want to
see this problem cleaned up once and for all. I can

arrange to supply you with a helicopter and ordnance. But if you and your boys do it, you're on your own."

Barrabas snickered. "We're on our own anyway."

"I'll be honest with you, Nile. Basically what I'm suggesting is that your perform an act of charity. I don't know what kind of paycheck you get from Uncle Sam for your 'unofficial' assignments. It's just that someone's got to take care of these pirate bastards, and my hands are tied."

"We get paid enough to do a few odd jobs in between."

Ryder shivered. "These are very cruel dudes you're messing with. Don't get captured. Know what I mean? I hear they're masters of the slow, painful death. If you say no, Nile, look—no hard feelings."

The two young Vietnamese girls, Linh and An, had impressed Barrabas. It wasn't because of what they'd endured. It was the fact that they *had* endured it, clinging tenaciously to life in the face of unspeakable pain and humiliation.

If the world needed heroes, it had only to look at those two young girls in the refugee camp waiting for a country to give them a new home. There was a personal motivation for accepting Ryder's offer, too. Barrabas hated being beaten. It left him with a sour taste in his mouth, and something more—the fear of hitting a losing streak.

Maybe it was just a mercenary's superstition, but every fiber of his body told him that if he didn't get out there and work on the score, it would eat away at him.

Ryder cleared his throat after the men had ridden in silence for a while. "So what are you thinking?"

Barrabas looked at him with a half smile. "I'm thinking I'll ask the boys. And I've got a feeling this is right up their alley. I sure as hell know it's right up mine."

4

In all directions the sea ended at the horizon. The Asian sun beat down relentlessly as a sixty-foot fishing boat steamed steadily across the turquoise waves. It headed toward a second, larger trawler half a kilometer off. A strange half-human, tigerlike creature, painted in garish colors along the hull of the trawler, appeared to breathe fire. The slashing, curved letters of the Thai alphabet spelled out the ship's name—the *Blood Maiden*. Flagship of the Red Vengeance.

Ki Lim stood on the bridge of the smaller boat, watching carefully as it pulled alongside the trawler. His sailors, short, wiry Asians, sprang to secure the two boats. Their sweating half-naked bodies were bronzed and roughened by wind and sun and scrawled with elaborate spiraling tattoos.

Ki Lim slowly crossed the hemp bridge to the *Blood Maiden*. He walked smoothly, holding his head high. His eyes and mouth were impassive but slightly cruel. A sailor ran toward him and bowed in oriental deference.

"Great Leader Hum Lo desires the presence of Ki Lim," the man said, bowing deeply once again.

"I will come to him now, Chung Hee," Ki Lim replied as he turned toward the stern of the ship, where the bridge and sailors' quarters rose above the forest of winches and radar antennae. The steel doors of the cargo hold had been pulled aside, and the sounds of weeping and the occasional groan rose to the deck. Ki Lim stopped as he passed, casually looking over the edge into the darkness.

The bright sunlight bled across the bodies of more than a dozen Vietnamese women, their legs manacled together with iron rings on a long, heavy chain. They wept, some alone, some with their heads buried for comfort on one another's shoulders.

Ki Lim watched for several moments. One of the women, noticing the long shadow cast into her prison from the deck above, looked up and caught his eye. She was probably little more than fifteen. She made him shiver.

"A new load of whores," Chung Hee explained, coming up behind Ki Lim. "We took another boat of refugees last night."

"And the rest of the refugees? What happened to them?"

"They were set free after we relieved them of their gold and their most beautiful women."

"They should have been killed."

"The Great Leader has decided," Chung Hee said cautiously. Then he shrugged. "Of course, they had no food or water left."

"That one there." Ki Lim pointed to the woman looking up at them, her tear-stained face wrought with fear. "She has blue eyes."

"Undoubtedly the bastard daughter of some American soldier."

"She interests me."

Chung Hee raised his hand in alarm. "Hum Lo has not yet taken his choice. And already two sailors who did not wait are feeling his wrath, Ki Lim."

The pirate shifted in annoyance and looked at Chung Hee. "I am well aware that they belong first to the Great Leader. He is most generous with the fruits of our victories."

Chung Hee bowed deeply once more. "And you, Ki Lim, who will someday be our next Great Leader, and who will someday not want for the woman of your choice, will surely be equally generous in your time."

"Chung Hee, there is some information I want."

"I am anxious to be of use."

"There is a military man, probably an American, very tall with nearly white hair and blue eyes. He is part of a military task force, a commando group, undoubtedly based in Songkhla. I want to know everything about him. Have our people bring us the information."

Wordlessly Ki Lim turned away from Chung Hee and the spectacle of the enslaved women. As he moved toward the captain's quarters, he reflected that Hum Lo would not last forever.

The Great Leader of the Red Vengeance was getting soft. To be a pirate in the China Sea required an ultimate degree of ruthlessness. He, Ki Lim, possessed that virtue. Hum Lo no longer did, and that would bring the pirates of the Red Vengeance great trouble someday.

Hum Lo's quarters were one level below deck at the stern of the *Blood Maiden*. Two pirates, the Great Leader's faithful guard dogs, stood outside the closed doors. They wore trousers and military style khaki shirts, but their sinewy biceps were bound with gold armlets. The gold chains around their necks were strung with tiny scapulary.

"The Great Leader does not wish to be disturbed," one of the guards said.

Chung Hee bowed. "The Great Leader, in his infinite wisdom, makes righteous decisions. However, he has requested the presence of his faithful servant Ki Lim, who has just arrived from his latest mission."

The guard eyed them coldly. "Hum Lo consults the oracle. He has given us his orders."

Ki Lim bristled. He was second only to the Great Leader in the hierarchy of the Red Vengeance. The guard's arrogance angered him. As for the oracle, he had little use for that silly old man.

Suddenly the sounds of shouts burst from behind the door, followed quickly by breaking glass. The other guard turned with alarm just as the door opened. A wizened Asian swathed in brightly colored robes scurried through, his arms folded around his head for protection. He was followed by flying projectiles and the shouts and curses of the Great Leader. An empty bottle and several brass goblets slammed against the wall in the corridor.

The guard went into Hum Lo's quarters and closed the door. The little man breathed a sigh of relief and smoothed his strange robes. Ki Lim and Chung Hee stared at him in amazement.

"The Great Leader, in his wisdom, blames the messenger for the bad news," he explained.

"Do the stars configure badly?" Ki Lim asked. The little old man was adept at reading the messages written in the night sky and in understanding the other daily omens that ruled the lives of the superstitious pirates.

"I am only the mouthpiece of the gods," the old man said humbly. "I tell what I see. I do not arrange it."

"Are the omens bad?" Ki Lim demanded again.

The Chinese soothsayer bowed. "Great One," he addressed Ki Lim. "Mars, the god of war, passes close to the horse and his rider, which is the double star at the top corner of the Great Dipper. This is troublesome. The pirates of the Red Vengeance are restless. Great projects are best delayed."

"Is that all?" Ki Lim demanded.

The astrologer looked uncomfortable, but said nothing.

"Tell me!" Ki Lim grabbed the man by the folds of cloth at his neck. The little man jumped, alarm leaping into his eyes.

"No! No, there is more. I will tell you, Great One."

"Then tell!" Ki Lim ordered. With one arm, he pulled the little man up, holding him on the tips of his toes.

"There are omens," he said, his eyes growing wide and his voice lowering to a bare whisper. "Terrible, strange omens. I read the entrails of a pelican yesterday. They foretold terrible things."

"Go on!"

"Of the passing of one who has been great and powerful by another who is more powerful and greater still."

"You read all that in the entrails of a pelican!" Ki Lim laughed and dropped the soothsayer.

The old man smoothed his robes once again and looked offended. He backed away from Ki Lim. "There is more. There is a great star in the east that is suddenly growing dim. And another great star in the west has appeared. It has a long tail that sweeps across the sky, and it grows brighter.''

"And this new star does not augur well for the Red Vengeance?'' Again Ki Lim laughed.

The little man raised his finger. "I see the messages of the heavens as they are written, and with my humble skill I try to read them. All I have seen bodes ill for the Great Leader. Especially the new star. It is a great star, cold and white, greater even than the star of the east.''

Now the little man leaned forward, speaking into Ki Lim's ear, his voice barely audible.

"The Great Leader's time grows short. His light is dimmed by someone stronger, greater, someone whose light is blinding, and who will strike fear and terror in all who look on.'' Ki Lim felt a strange chill flutter up the back of his neck.

The door to Hum Lo's quarters opened, and the guard appeared. His face tightened into a scowl when he saw the soothsayer. "The Great Leader desires the presence of Ki Lim immediately.''

Quickly the old man leaned forward and pressed something into Ki Lim's hand, his lips once again passing close to the pirate's ear. "To save you from the evil eye. Remember, I am your servant.''

Ki Lim caught the little man's glance. Fear had left his eyes, which now twinkled with conspiracy. The little man pulled away. "Great Leader,'' he murmured, looking at Ki Lim before disappearing down the corridor.

Ki Lim looked at the tiny object in his hand. It was a silver eye with a shiny blue stone in the center. A blue eye. In Asian superstitions blue irises were a sign of the evil eye. He tucked it in his pocket and went in to meet the Great Leader. The dark-paneled room was dense with acrid incense. The Great Leader sat on an enormous divan, muttering and throwing handfuls of powder into a small charcoal brazier. A small electric ceiling fan quietly sucked away the smoke. He looked up as Ki Lim entered.

Hum Lo was an enormous man, weighing close to three hundred pounds. He rarely moved from his nest among the overstuffed pillows on the divan. On a small table in front of him stood bowls laden with fruits and nuts. His bushy eyebrows, which grew in a single line across his wide forehead, glowered darkly, but he welcomed Ki Lim with enthusiasm.

"Sit, sit, Ki Lim." He reached a thick arm for a flask of wine and filled a goblet on a nearby table, then handed it to the pirate. "Now tell me everything. Was the ship blown up?"

Ki Lim chose his words carefully. He had decided to omit all reference to the last-minute commando attack on the *Empress Christina*. Undoubtedly the attackers had themselves been surprised when the ship had blown up into a million pieces.

"The American government refused to meet the demands of the terrorists, so they gave the order to blow up the ship. With all hostages aboard."

"Yes. The shortwave radio has carried all the details. It is a pity about the hostages. So many innocent lives." Hum Lo sighed.

"I think not. It is dangerous to take prisoners. It is deadly to let them go free. There should never be witnesses. And last night? How many were on the refugee boat that you let go? They should have been drowned!"

"We have already discussed your penchant for killing, Ki Lim," Hum Lo said harshly, glaring to indicate the discussion was closed. "It was fortunate that they allowed you to leave before lighting the fuse." He slurped back a mouthful of wine. His fingers, fisted around the stem of his heavy goblet, were studded with thick gold rings. He looked at Ki Lim inquiringly and rubbed the side of his nose with his index finger. Hum Lo often had a self-satisfied look about him.

"Barely," Ki Lim replied. "I had to exit quietly at the last minute."

"How quietly?" Hum Lo asked. His lips twitched.

"This quietly." Ki Lim pulled his carbine from his belt and held it aloft. "Brother." He broke into a smile.

Hum Lo laughed. Uncontrollably.

"My brother! My friend!" The Great Leader held out one arm and beckoned for Ki Lim to sit. He socked back a great mouthful of wine, sputtering as he laughed and spilling it over his lips.

Ki Lim walked around the charcoal brazier toward the divan.

"Quite frankly, I don't like doing business with Mustafi Ali and his henchmen. They're much too volatile, my brother." He sat beside Hum Lo and drank deeply from the goblet he was offered.

"But they pay well, my brother," Hum Lo said as he handed Ki Lim a slip of paper. "A hundred thousand dollars deposited to your account in Zurich."

"And the other nine hundred thousand to your account?"

Hum Lo leaned back into his pillows and shrugged lightly. He reached for an apple on top of the fruit bowl. "I have expenses, dear brother. The ship, the crews, operating capital, bribes, you know. And I bartered for some of the amount. We now have launchers for heat-sensitive tracking missiles. We also have the missiles themselves."

"Congratulations, brother! Piracy is an expensive business these days," Ki Lim said as he nodded. "I see we have another batch of whores."

Hum Lo bit into the apple and chewed slowly. "Yes. Have any of them caught your eye? Last night two of the sailors got at them before I looked them over. They got a little rough with one of them. Killed her." He pinched his mouth in distaste and looked at the apple. "They will be punished tonight at the ceremonial dinner to celebrate victory over Mustafi Ali and the *Empress Christina.*"

"Victory?"

Hum Lo smiled and threw the apple aside. "One million dollars' worth. Which one do you want?" He picked out a date and started chewing again.

"The one with blue eyes."

Hum Lo stopped chewing and stared at Ki Lim. He pushed the date into his cheek. "Blue eyes are the sign of the evil eye, my brother. Are you sure you know what you are saying? The oracle was here, and he warned me. I was considering having the blue-eyed woman thrown overboard. Curse these American devils. They have infected our people."

"Surely, brother, you don't believe this silly hocus-pocus."

Hum Lo spat the date out. His blubbery body quivered as he turned angrily from Ki Lim.

"Yes, brother, I do. And you would well be warned to pay attention to the language of the heavens, too. The gods speak, and what they say to us must not be taken lightly."

"Bah." Ki Lim waved his arm in the air, dismissing the superstition. "We have moved far enough beyond these old ideas, with our ten-million-dollar trawlers and our heat-sensitive missiles. I would like to string the oracle from the bow by his toes. What did he say to you?''

Hum Lo turned away and spoke quietly. ''That the god of war is traveling. That one star fades while another grows bright. Greatness vanishes and is replaced.''

Ki Lim rose from the divan and paced. ''But these words could mean anything, Great Leader. The god of war is traveling? Then let it be us! We are war! The omen is a good one. It is time to launch our great adventure, Hum Lo. The god travels with us. As for these stars, perhaps they also mean something else. As the old star fades, so do old ideas, old ways of doing things. But this new star is even greater and brighter. We can be that brighter star—'' he grabbed Hum Lo by the shoulder and forced him to turn around ''—if we fight for it.''

The Great Leader looked at Ki Lim. It was not for nothing that he called him brother and had made him his second-in-command.

''You have an idea, Ki Lim?'' the Great Leader asked quietly. ''Tell me.''

''Seizing the *Empress Christina* was easy. A great luxury liner filled with hundreds of wealthy travelers. They put up less resistance than a refugee boat. We agreed to assist the terrorists in boarding for a million dollars. But why? There are millions aboard such ships in currency and jewels. Why help the terrorists? Why not help ourselves? There are hundreds of private yachts that frequent these waters each year, and we scarcely touch them.''

For a moment Hum Lo was silent. He slowly brushed his lips with his fingers and thought. He looked at Ki Lim.

''This intrigues me. I will think about it, and I will tell you what I think at the ceremonial dinner tonight. You may go.''

Ki Lim turned and walked toward the door. The Great Leader's voice stopped him.

''That girl you wanted. Take her. She's yours.''

Ki Lim smiled graciously. ''Thank you, brother.'' He opened the door and stepped outside, but once again Hum Lo called out.

''Ki Lim!''

The pirate turned to his leader.

''Beware of blue eyes!'' Hum Lo smiled slightly and turned back to his bowl of fruit.

5

The port area of Songkhla was a steamy neighborhood of crowded buildings and narrow streets. By night it was almost entirely deserted except for the occasional café where the doors were tightly shut and short Asian men in expensive suits watched from behind barred windows. Closer to the water, the neighborhood opened on an esplanade lined with noisy taverns and food counters where old women labored over pots of steaming vegetables.

Lee Hatton had a rendezvous in one of these taverns. Barrabas had called a meeting and had given the mercs instructions on how to get there.

She walked quickly through dark empty streets as she made her way from the modern hotel on the other side of the town's old stone fortress. It had rained for an hour that afternoon, a thick tropical rain accompanied by heaving thunder. When it ended, the sun emerged long enough to turn the newly fallen moisture into steam.

Occasionally a window opened in an upper story, casting a square of dim light onto the wet pavement.

A man or woman looked out, then quickly closed the shutter and the street fell into darkness again.

Lee took a handkerchief from the pocket of her khaki slacks and wiped her forehead. She pulled the clammy cotton fabric of her tan shirt from her breasts and arms. Her mother had told her once that animals sweat, men perspire and ladies glow. But this woman is sweating, thought Lee, like a pig in a smokehouse. In this climate breathing constituted heavy exertion.

Her ears picked up another sound. Footsteps— down the street. Someone was walking behind her and picking up speed. She listened carefully. She could estimate a hundred and forty pounds. She tensed when she felt someone's hand on her elbow. She swung her arm up, her hand flat like a blade, when she heard a woman's worried voice.

"Can I walk with you?" The blond American woman gasped and stepped back at the sight of Lee's half-raised karate chop. She was young, in her early twenties, and quite beautiful. She wore expensive blue slacks and a light silk blouse. The wicker handbag made a tempting target for thieves.

Lee's face broke into a welcoming smile. "Sorry. I heard you coming. But in the Far East your footsteps could as easily have been a man's."

"I'm sorry I surprised you. It's so dark, and you have short, dark hair. I couldn't tell if you were a man or woman either. I think some men were following me, and I got frightened. Can I walk with you? At least till we're out of this neighborhood?''

"No problem. Where are you going? Are you lost or something? Name's Lee, by the way. Lee Hatton.''

The woman nodded. "Drew. Nancy Drew Stevens. But everybody calls me Drew. My mother loved mystery stories. I'm traveling around the world with my father and my fiancé on Dad's boat. We're from San Francisco. I went shopping and got lost in this neighborhood on my way back to the harbor. They'll be worried about me.'' The two women started walking again.

"Are you sure you were being followed?'' Lee asked.

"I don't know if they were following or not. There were three men behind me about a hundred feet, and every time I turned into another street, they were there, too. When I started walking faster to catch up to you, they disappeared into an alleyway.''

"You were being followed," Lee said matter-of-factly. "Do you know how to defend yourself?''

"I have this.'' Drew reached into her handbag and pulled out a little aerosol can of Mace.

"Handy," Lee admitted, privately thinking that if three men had attacked this woman, Mace would probably have got her nothing but more trouble.

"Was that a karate chop you almost gave me?'' Drew asked slowly.

"Sure was. My late father was a U.S. Army general who wanted a son instead of a daughter. He made the best of it, though. I was well trained, and I've known how to take care of myself since before I can remember."

They reached the end of a row of buildings and stepped across a wide puddle at the curb. Suddenly three short Asian men moved from the shadows of the dark side street, fanning out and blocking their escape.

"Oh, God, it's them!" Drew turned white and backed against the wall.

The thieves eyed the two women and laughed quickly among themselves. One of the men pointed at Drew's purse and jabbered instructions. They leered and closed in. Bicycle chains, wound around their palms, were raised aloft.

"Got your Mace, honey?" Lee muttered under her breath to Drew. The young woman nodded, speechless with fear. "Then use it on the guy to your right. *Now!*"

Drew held up a trembling arm and pushed the nozzle on the spray can. The noxious chemical spewed forth, fouling the air with its pepperlike odor. The man on the right screamed and put up his hands to shield his eyes. Bravely Drew took a step toward him, spraying the Mace over his body.

The other two attacked.

Lee kicked to the side and straight up, connecting with the chin of the man on her far left. His teeth shattered as his jawbone fell lose from its hinge. The one in the middle swung his chain.

The words went through Lee's cool and collected mind just as she had learned them years before. A chain defense demands speed and agility. Don't let the attacker get too much momentum. Don't let the chain gather too much speed. She reacted, ducking and letting the chain swing past her. Then she jumped forward, grabbing the attacker's wrist while it was still in the air. She swerved behind him, using the back of her body as a lever against his back and locking his arm over her left shoulder.

With a single hard, downward jerk, she bent his arm back and broke his elbow. As her attacker screamed in agony, she let go, pushing him away. His arm hung uselessly at his side, the lower arm swinging at a wild angle from the elbow. The chain was on the ground.

Shrieks and the sound of running feet came from the side street. The boys had friends. Two more men came whipping out of the shadows. Drew aimed her little can of Mace and pressed the activator. Nothing came out. Tears poured down her face, and she started coughing.

Lee moved in front of Drew just as another bicycle chain came her way. It slapped across Lee's shoulder, leaving a stinging streak on her skin. She backed away, and when the man swung his arm back, Lee moved in.

She bent her arms up in front of her and slid in close with a double forearm block to his arm. The chain flew past her as she swung her right leg up into his groin and slammed her elbow in his ribs.

Two more seconds to finish him off, and she'd be on to the next.

But the next was on to her, his bicycle chain whipping down over her shoulder and the side of her face. He dropped the chain, and a knife flashed in his other hand. He drove it toward her heart.

Suddenly a big hand came out of the blue, slapping down across the knifer's neck and jerking him back. He sailed into the air.

Lee brought the side of her hand down across the neck of her man. There was a solid crack as his neck broke and his limp body dropped.

Lee looked up in time to see Barrabas slam the knife man into the wall. The other attackers picked themselves up and ran, and the knife man jumped up to join them. Barrabas gave him a head start with the steel toe of his boot planted squarely in the rear end. The man sailed three feet into the air and landed on his face, then he jumped up and tore off like a bat out of hell.

"You okay?" Lee turned to Drew, panting to catch her breath.

Drew nodded, white and frightened.

"Colonel, you always show up at the best times," Lee said to Barrabas.

"Was that a date, or were you just cruising?" Barrabas asked wryly. He toed the body of the man with the broken neck. There was no movement. He was dead.

"Momma always told me not to flirt with strangers," Lee replied. "This is Drew Stevens. They were following her earlier, and I guess when they saw me they decided to double their pleasure. What are you doing in this neighborhood?"

"The tavern is just a block away. How's your hand, Lee?"

"Sore," she replied, shaking it. "And my skin will heal, but damn, they ruined this shirt." She pointed to two long, greasy rips down the sleeve and back.

"The police can answer their own questions about this creep." He nodded to the body sprawled at his feet. "Let's get out of here."

THE TEMPERATURE IN THE DARK, humid hold of the *Blood Maiden* was over a hundred degrees. For three days now twenty young Vietnamese women had huddled there, sweating and sobbing. Their cries of terror broke from their unsettled sleep as they encountered their fate in dreams.

The door to the hold slid back. It was night. A spotlight was beamed down, and pirates descended a rope ladder. The women held their hands to their eyes to block out the sudden painful brightness. One girl was chosen to empty the brimming bucket of excrement. Another was told to hand out the meager rations of rice and warm, stale water. If they didn't move fast enough—and sometimes just for the sport of their jailers—they were slapped or kicked.

The pirates, their bodies foul-smelling and tattooed, stood over the young women, leering and joking as they pointed to the ones who caught their eye. When the women were fed and watered, the pirates left, muttering their unintelligible jokes and laughing. The door to the stinking, fetid hold was closed, and total darkness fell around them once again.

Lac Sam finished her tiny bowl of sour rice and bunched her legs up against her chest. Once again she waited. Twice a day the sailors came. Twice a day the terrible monotony of their prison was broken by sunlight and fresh air. Twice a day the women trembled at the feet of their captors, never knowing if this time they would be singled out for rape or something worse.

The young Vietnamese girl clenched her arms around her knees and pulled farther into a corner away from the others. Nearby a woman sobbed uncontrollably. She had been sobbing like that for three days now. Lac Sam closed her eyes and waited for the pirates to come again.

Her dream was fitful, the recurrent images sometimes blurring over one another. Her mother waved to her from the little marketplace stall in Ho Chi Minh City. Suddenly she was gone, replaced by a crowd of schoolchildren, taunting her, pointing their fingers at her, laughing and running away. In her dream she was filled with loneliness and sorrow. It was not her fault that she had been born with blue eyes, that blue was the color of the evil eye.

Her mother appeared before her again and talked to her. She told Lac Sam that her father was an American soldier. He was so tall that he stood as high as the gingko trees that grew along the boulevards of the old city. He had a smile, her mother told her, like the sunrise in the morning that made the bluebirds sing. He was handsome and good to her, and one day, before Lac Sam was even born, he went away and never came back.

When the other children made fun of her, or rejected her because of her blue eyes, her mother always said, "Don't worry, Lac Sam. Someday you will go to America where everyone has blue eyes."

In the stinking hold of the *Blood Maiden*, Lac Sam dreamed she was in America, the land of giants. She stood in the middle of a great city of big buildings, with tall people and enormous cars rushing past. Then, far down the street, she saw him—her American father with his blue eyes. He walked toward her. He was smiling. She felt safe.

Suddenly the dream image was shattered by darkness and an icy, cold wind that made Lac Sam's sleeping body shudder. Her dying mother pressed into her hand the gold coins she had hidden from the communists and told her eighteen-year-old daughter to go to America. Soft moans escaped Lac Sam's lips as her sleep was torn by memories. Under cover of darkness, the boat with its precious cargo of eighty refugees slipped down the river past the deadly Vietnamese army guards. At the coast another boat appeared mysteriously beside them. The navigator, who had arranged everything and had taken their gold, abruptly left them. They discovered that no one on board knew how to sail, or where they were going. Somehow they managed, following the stars as they sailed west, and the next day, following the movement of the sun.

Then the storm came. For two days they alternated between paralyzing nausea and a searing weariness after bailing water from the leaky boat as strong winds and high waves threatened to capsize them. The storm ended as abruptly as it had begun. On the morning of the fourth day, the sun rose, hot and golden over a calm, windless ocean.

They floated two more days, their ragged sails limp as the last of their food and water ran out. They prayed to their ancestors for salvation. Finally, on that last afternoon, they saw a ship far off on the horizon.

The refugees ran to the side of the boat, shouting and waving blankets to attract attention. Cheers of thanksgiving and joy rose into the air as the trawler came closer. The cheers died when the terrible painting on the bow of the ship became visible.

The boat people were puzzled. The symbols and alphabet were foreign to them, yet ominous. A sense of evil pervaded. The ship loomed closer until its bow shadowed over the little refugee boat. Motor launches filled with men were lowered over the side of the trawler. They tore through the water, pulling alongside the rickety Vietnamese craft.

"Pirates!" someone shrieked in realization. But it was already too late. They attacked. Naked, sweaty men covered with tattoos streamed over the sides of the boat, beating and pillaging as they went, killing all who resisted. The girls were dragged forward and thrown into the launches. A young woman refused to be separated from her baby. A pirate grabbed the infant by the legs and slammed its head against the side of the boat. The baby split open like a ripe apple and was flung overboard.

A teenage boy tried to defend his sister. He was dragged forward by his hair. A pirate with a machete severed the boy's head with one mighty blow.

Lac Sam jumped from her dream, strangling the scream that had been building in her throat. She opened her eyes, facing the claustrophobic darkness of the hold again. Somewhere another girl was already screaming.

Lac Sam moved through the pitch-black toward her, careful not to trip over the long chain locked to her ankle. She put her arms around the tortured girl to comfort her.

When the women had been put aboard the pirates' trawler, some of them had turned on her, blaming Lac Sam with her evil blue eyes for their troubles. In the darkness of the *Blood Maiden* no one recoiled from her. Her eyes were invisible. The sobbing girl in her arms needed comfort, however anonymous. The women knew what was in store for them.

On the first night of their imprisonment, two of the pirates, reeking of alcohol and carrying bottles of rice wine, had come to the hold. They had chosen one of the girls and had laughed as they had raped her. When she had begun to bleed, they had laughed harder and had raped her again. They had beaten her until other pirates had come and dragged away their drunken comrades.

The young girl had died in a lake of her own blood. Lac Sam and another woman had been ordered to carry the body onto the deck and throw it overboard.

The shrill scream of metal rollers sliding on rusty metal tracks twisted up and down Lac Sam's backbone. Above her, the hold door slid open, revealing a square of velvet night sky set with diamond stars.

The rope ladder was flung down. The dark, leering faces of pirates appeared over the edge.

Lac Sam caught her breath, and the young girl in her arms clutched at her shoulders.

It wasn't time for food and water.

That meant it was time for something terrible.

Several of the pirates descended into the hold with flashlights. They strolled silently among the prisoners, shining their lights on them. A woman recoiled and backed away, shielding her face. Two of the pirates grabbed her and pulled her forward, holding her up to the flashlight of the third pirate. He shook his head. The woman was thrown back against the wall. The pirates went on, their occasional comments followed by low chuckles.

Lac Sam closed her eyes and prayed to her ancestors, especially to the unknown ancestors of the American father she had never seen. She asked them for courage and strength to survive. The girl in her arms whimpered and clung closer. She felt the blinding yellow light beating against her eyelids. She opened her eyes and stared back.

"That one!" the pirate said, uttering his words with a satisfied smile. "Take her!"

The two sailors went forward, but stopped when Lac Sam stared steadily at them.

"Go on! Take her! Or Ki Lim will have your ears!" the man with the flashlight shouted.

Reluctantly the two pirates reached out and grabbed Lac Sam, pushing the other girl away.

One of the pirates unlocked the ankle cuff that held her to the chain. The man with the flashlight looked her over. He grabbed the collar of her blouse and ripped it from her body with a powerful sweep of his arm. He chuckled.

"Put it on her," he said to one of the others.

Another pirate came forward with a leather collar and snapped it around her neck.

"Ki Lim will amuse himself with this pet," the man with the flashlight said.

One of the other pirates nodded reluctantly, then mumbled, "But the eyes. She should be put overboard before she lays a curse upon the *Blood Maiden* and the Red Vengeance. She should be killed."

The man with the flashlight laughed. "When Ki Lim finishes with his women, they are put overboard. And if they're not already dead, they soon drown." He plucked her chin between his finger and thumb and held her face up to his. "And if you have not met death by then, Blue Eyes, you will be praying for it to come swiftly."

6

Barrabas and Hatton walked the young American woman to a wharf not far from the tavern. A sleek sixty-foot schooner rested at anchor beside the wharf, and they waited until Drew had boarded before turning back to the esplanade along the harbor.

The sidewalks were jammed with small Thais jostling and shoving in every direction. In the street, food sellers labored over gas-fired woks and shouted their specialities. Little men with their arms strung with gold watches darted furtively along the sidelines, picking out tourists.

"Lady, I have good Rolex. Very good. Big mister, you buy for little lady?" Barrabas shook his head and pushed through the crowd.

"If those were real, he wouldn't have twenty of them strung up and down his arm," Hatton remarked.

"It's over there," Barrabas said, pointing to the double doors of a bar that opened onto the busy sidewalk.

"How'd you find this place?" Lee asked.

"I didn't. Nanos and Beck were away from their hotel when I set this up, but Claude told me they were meeting him here this evening. I figured we could all meet here. By the way, how's Claude's hand?"

"The bone was a little chipped, and it'll be sore for a while, but he'll be able to use it in a few days. Why? You think he'll need it?"

"Could be." Barrabas was evasive. He checked his sleeve to make sure it was pulled down over the tattoo. Why in hell had he done it? he asked himself for the umpteenth time that day. Tattoos drew people's attention. It was the last thing he wanted.

They stepped through the doors into a long, smoky room, dense with loud, animated conversation. It was a men's tavern filled with sailors, stevedores and traders of every race and nationality. At a glance it was obvious why Nanos and Beck had chosen it for their Songkhla pub crawl. The tiny Thai barmaids, tipping their way delicately through the mob with their full, heavy trays in the air, were topless.

The mercs had gathered at a table not far from the front doors. A little waitress stood nervously beside the table, with Alex Nanos towering over her. He lifted four great mugs of foamy beer from her tray and placed them on the table in front of Nate Beck, Claude Hayes and Geoff Bishop. Billy Two sat slightly to one side, looking sullen and dissatisfied.

"Awright, it's the Colonel and Lee!" the Greek crowed when his eyes lit on the newcomers. "Couple more beer, there," he instructed the barmaid. Alex Nanos was already three sheets to the wind. If the mercs had been on assignment, it would have been the end of the line for him. But until Barrabas presented them with Ryder's information and they made their own decisions, they were entitled to spend their R & R the way each saw fit.

"Uh-uh, forget it," Barrabas said quickly, waving away a glass of beer. He pulled a chair out for Lee and sat beside her.

"What in hell happened to you?" Bishop exclaimed, seeing the woman's torn shirt.

"Funny thing happened on the way to the tavern..." Lee laughed nervously and began telling them the story.

Barrabas turned to Billy Two. The massive, barrel-chested Osage rarely looked more morose.

"What's the matter, Billy?" Barrabas asked.

Billy Two looked up at him with big brown doll's eyes that spoke of sorrow.

"I can't get over the *Empress Christina*. All those dead people. Alex, Nate, the rest of them, they all forget about it and go on with life. Me, I feel terrible. I just can't help feeling we weren't fast enough."

"There was nothing we could've done differently," Barrabas assured him. "I didn't like it either. But we may have a chance to make up for it."

Billy Two's eyes wandered down to the colonel's rolled-up shirtsleeve. "Tattoo?" he asked.

"Shhh." The other mercs were listening to Lee. Barrabas quickly lifted the sleeve and pulled it back down. "Don't ask..." he said.

Starfoot just folded his great arms across his massive chest and nodded his head. "It's a good one. Heap powerful Thai war god."

He was interrupted by Geoff Bishop, the Canadian airman, as Lee Hatton finished telling her story to the others.

"I can't believe you both just let the rest of them go!" he said angrily. I'd have..."

"Yeah, Bishop?" Nanos interrupted loudly. He jumped to his feet aggressively. "You couldn't..."

"They won't bother anyone," Barrabas cut in. "Not the way Lee took care of them. Especially the dead one. Alex, sit down."

Nanos slowly sat. The mercs were uncomfortably silent a moment.

"Besides, I didn't feel like hanging around to answer questions when the police got there," Lee said, breaking the chill.

Nate Beck laughed. "Yeah. They're probably friends of the bad guys anyway."

"There's another problem I want to fill you in on." Barrabas pulled his chair forward and addressed them seriously. He told them of his visit to the refugee camp earlier that day and explained

Commander Ryder's idea of the connection between the Red Vengeance and the annihilation of the *Empress Christina*.

"So they want us to go after pirates, do they?" Bishop mused out loud when Barrabas had finished. "How?"

"It'll all be done unofficially. But Ryder promised me air power. An armed helicopter. You'll have to fly it, if you agree to do this."

There was a momentary silence before Hayes spoke in his long, Southern drawl. "Well, hell. I always like to do some charity in between jobs, Colonel. I can't speak for the others, but I have the feeling they're going to go along with it."

Around the table, Nate Beck, Billy Two and Nanos were nodding.

Lee shuddered. "And they think there's some kind of slave trade in these Vietnamese boat women. Now I wonder if those guys tonight were after Drew's purse or..."

"Very little is known about the Red Vengeance, although there are lots of gruesome stories," Barrabas explained. "They move around on the sea, hiding out in islands in the Gulf of Thailand, or sometimes in isolated ports on the mainland. Their leader is Chinese, name of Hum Lo. There are stories that he keeps a stable of women and rewards his sailors with gifts of their services."

Nanos leaned back on his chair, chewing a tooth-pick, his hands clasped behind his head. "So all we gotta do is catch the Red Vengeance red-handed."

Barrabas nodded. "That's about the size of it. What do you say?"

"Count me in," Nanos answered quickly.

"Me, too," Beck added.

A chorus of assent came from around the table.

Suddenly the Greek's voice rose above the others, "Hey, all right." He rocked forward on his chair and leaped to his feet as Drew Stevens tentatively approached the table. An older man with graying hair accompanied her.

"Howdy do, miss...? My name's Alex, but they call me The Greek. Have you...?"

Drew smiled graciously at Alex and turned to Lee and Barrabas. "Actually, my father wanted to meet you after I told him what happened." The older man pushed his way through and thrust out his hand.

"Theodorus Stevens," he said, proudly. "Captain of the good ship *Diogenes*. And I understand I owe my daughter's life to some people here."

Barrabas stood. "The credit goes to Lee," he said, gesturing toward the woman merc.

Drew's father reached inside his shirt and pulled out a thick wallet. "As a token of my gratitude, I want you to take this...." He pulled out several hundred-dollar bills.

Lee almost laughed. She put her hands up and pushed the money and the wallet away. "I don't need it, really I don't. And if you flash that kind of cash around here, you're really asking for trouble."

On the other side of the table, Nanos was still trying to get Drew's attention.

"Take it easy, Alex. Take it easy," Nate Beck cajoled. "She's probably got a boyfriend."

"No way, man. Look at her. Only the Greek knows how to give her what she wants."

The other mercs had risen from the table and were getting ready to pull out. The decision to go after the Red Vengeance meant a major change in plans for all of them. The after-mission blowout was over. Instinctively the mercs started sobering up in preparation for the days ahead.

There was one thing Nanos hadn't had in his time off, though, and it was still the main thing on his mind.

"You think with your balls, Alex," Billy Two commented solemnly. The Greek couldn't take his eyes off Drew.

"Yeah?" Alex replied insolently. "I shoot with them, too. I'm a package deal. Look at that guy." Nate followed Alex's eyes. Geoff Bishop was moving around to stand beside Lee Hatton, who was still engrossed in conversation with Drew Stevens and her father.

"What about it?" Beck asked.

"As if moving in on Lee Hatton wasn't enough for him, now he's moving in on the blond babe."

"Nahh, Alex." Nate Beck was clearly exasperated.

"You think too much, Alex," Billy Two told the Greek. "It makes you jealous."

Claude Hayes looked at Billy Two skeptically. "Really? I didn't know Alex could think. He's got the responses of a bull moose in heat."

"He thinks," Nate Beck said. "That's what's worrying me right now. It makes him dangerous."

Alex pushed away from the others and moved to where Drew and her father were standing with Lee Hatton, Bishop and Barrabas. He flexed his shoulders as he sidled up beside Drew. "Hi, there. I thought maybe I could offer to show you the sights of Songkhla."

Drew laughed. "I think I've pretty much seen what I want to. There's not much here besides the old fort. Thanks anyway."

"But, baby," Nanos said plaintively. "I'm the main attraction. Maybe we can get to know each other."

"Alex—" Lee moved in and put her hand on his shoulder "—the lady said no thanks. Drew and her father—and her fiancé—are leaving on their boat for Borneo early in the morning. We've got a job tomorrow, too."

Barrabas and Hatton walked with the two civilians toward the door of the crowded tavern.

Nanos's eyes followed Drew's curvaceous body. The Greek was dark and tense. Disappointment made his fever turn cold.

"Come on, Alex," Nate urged, seeing the change come over his buddy. "You've had a lot to drink, and we're back on the job now. Let's go find the hotel and dry out."

"Yeah," Billy Two agreed. "I've seen you look like this before, Alex. And I know what happens next. Let's go before it does." He put his hand on Nanos's shoulder to urge him toward the door.

Alex pulled away angrily. "Stop treating me like a goddamn kid. I'll do what the hell I want."

"Shit," Starfoot cursed, and turned to Beck. "Like I said, I've seen it before."

Nanos's eyes lit upon Geoff Bishop, who was talking with Claude Hayes. "I saw the way that fucker looked at the blond chick. Hey, Bishop!"

Before Nate or Billy Two could react, Alex took three long, half-running paces toward the Canadian pilot. His right arm flew up and his fist plowed toward Bishop's face.

Bishop saw it coming. He whipped around, blocking with his left and balling his right fist for the comeback. The eyes of the rivals froze together with icy hatred in their momentary stalemate. Claude

Hayes shoved between Nanos and Bishop, pushing their fists aside.

Billy Two and Nate Beck closed in quickly on the rampaging Greek, grabbing his arms. Nanos struggled to push them off, throwing himself at Bishop. Hayes drew up his beefy forearms, pushing Nanos away. He blocked Bishop with his massive back.

The Greek went red in the face, the veins in his forehead and down his arms swelling mightily as the adrenaline poured into his body. "I'll take your fucking head off, Bishop!" he roared, throwing himself forward again.

Starfoot's and Beck's arms held him firmly, and the two mercs dragged Nanos backward. The Greek kicked and struggled against their grip.

"I'm going to punch his fucking head in," Bishop swore, and tried to edge around Claude Hayes. Nanos was struggling against the hold of his two friends several feet away. The two men clawed toward each other.

"Uh-uh," Hayes said in a forbidding bass voice. He shoved up against Bishop and pushed the man back. "Just ease off. The guy's had too much to drink."

"The guy's an asshole," Bishop said bitterly. "I've had all I can take from him."

"Man, we all know the Greek's been on your case too long. Just cool it. We're your buddies, too. We'll take care of it."

The ripples of the violent confrontation swept quickly through the tavern. Men rose at other tables, jeering and egging the fight on. Some of them were waiting for the first opportunity to join in. A heavyset bouncer was moving down the bar with feline wariness.

"Quick! Get him in there!" Billy Two told Beck, jerking his head toward the nearby door to the toilets.

They swung Nanos around as the Greek strained and shouted obscenities. Beck stuck out a foot and kicked open the door as Nanos arched forward to throw them off. The three men flew into the washroom and landed in a heap on the floor.

Nanos jumped up and headed back for the door, but the alcohol had slowed his reflexes. He still had brute strength from his muscular body, but no agility or coordination. Nate Beck grabbed his arm, and Nanos swung around and slugged his friend, his fist glancing off Beck's chin and knocking his head back. He grabbed Beck by the shirt with both hands.

"Holy shit, Billy, he's gone nuts!" Beck shouted. The Greek's eyes glowed with feral intensity.

Billy Two reached out a long, thick arm and grabbed Nanos under the armpit and around the chest. Nanos slammed his fists into the Osage's chest. It was like slugging a tree trunk. Billy Two kicked open the door to a cubicle and pulled the chain on the wall. The toilet flushed.

"Nate!" he shouted. He handed Beck the chain. "Keep flushing!" Ice-cold water poured from the overhead tank into the toilet. "Take a ride on the porcelain bus, Alex!" Billy Two shouted, almost gleefully. With two massive hands, the Indian turned the Greek upside down and stuck him headfirst in the bowl.

Nanos's blue shrieks of anger died in the loud splutter of cold water. He twisted and kicked to free himself from Billy's iron-tight hold, but Nate Beck moved in and grabbed the other arm. They pulled his head up. Nanos sucked back air.

"You gotta cool off, guy!" Beck shouted angrily.

"Fuck you!" Nanos screamed.

Beck pulled the chain again, and once more they plunged the Greek's head into the bowl and held it there.

"One more time," Beck said to Billy Two. They pulled him up for air and sent him back down to the water before he had a chance to curse them. This time his eyes were glazing over. When they brought him up a third time, Alex was tame.

"You bastards," he spluttered through the water streaming down his face. "You're supposed to be a guy's friend...."

"Come on, Alex," Nate Beck said gently as he and Billy Two helped the Greek to his feet. "Let's go back to the hotel. You've got to cool down."

Nanos was dazed as the two mercs helped him out of the narrow cubicle.

"Man, it's going to take a heap of work to make this up to Bishop." Billy Two shook his head sagely.

Alex curled his lips, and his breath came in short jerks. "I'll get that bastard," he swore.

"Alex..." Billy Two began.

Suddenly Nanos jumped for the door. "No, man, forget it!" he yelled. The two mercs reached out to grab him again. The door to the room was flung open, and Barrabas filled the frame just as Alex got there.

The Greek looked surprised. The colonel reached back and swung forward. His big fist slammed hard into the side of Nanos's face. The Greek looked even more surprised. He careened backward into Nate's and Billy Two's arms. Nanos stared up at the colonel, rubbing his painful jaw.

Barrabas glared at him. "You're a jerk, Alex. Let's hope Bishop is there to cover your ass if the Red Vengeance gives us trouble. Because every man in this unit depends on the other guy for his life. Let's hope Bishop forgets about this. Because if he doesn't, you've just put all of us in jeopardy."

The white-haired colonel turned to leave, but swung around sharply to face the astonished Greek once more. He pointed his finger, and his lips tightened in anger. "You do that ever again, Nanos—and you're out."

7

Naked and humiliated, Lac Sam was pushed along
the deck toward the stern of the *Blood Maiden*. Pirate seamen turned from their jobs, laughing and
making rude gestures. Occasionally the man leading
her flicked the long chain attached to her leather
collar, causing her to falter and stumble. The roars
and hoots of derision grew stronger and louder.

The ship was lit festively, with tiny bulbs glowing
up and down the mast and cranes. The moon, one
day past full, glowed brightly on the calm China Sea.
Dozens of smaller fishing boats rested gently at
anchor in the waters around the *Blood Maiden*.

Lac Sam tried desperately not to look left or right
and hid her body as best she could with her hands.
But other, sea-roughened hands reached from the
terrible gauntlet to pull her arms aside. She had never
known humiliation until this.

The staterooms and cabins at the stern of the
Blood Maiden were brilliantly lit at every porthole.
As Lac Sam drew near, she heard the sounds of men
singing and cascades of laughter from within. At the

door, the pirate leading her stopped and held her back. With a malicious smile, he opened the door and flung her through with a hard push.

Lac Sam tripped and fell facedown inside the room. The laughter rose to a deafening crescendo, then slowly died. She felt the chain tugging at her collar. Trembling with shame and fear, she began to push herself up from the floor.

But not fast enough.

Her captor jerked the leash hard. Lac Sam gurgled and coughed as the collar tightened around her trachea. She fell on her backside and stared up into the roomful of mocking eyes.

There were perhaps fifty men there, Chinese and Thai, the captains of all the Red Vengeance ships. They sat before long, low tables that held gleaming silver dishes laden with food. Over Western trousers and shirts, they wore robes of red and blue brocade woven heavily with gold threads.

Servers, dressed in black oriental pajamas, moved swiftly and furtively behind the pirate captains of the Red Vengeance, replenishing empty dishes and wine goblets and disappearing through swinging doors that led to the kitchens beyond.

At the end of the room, at a table set perpendicular to the others, Hum Lo sat with Ki Lim and other favorites. He rose slowly from his cushions, heaving his great bulk upward with effort and adjusting the sleeves of his blood-red robe. Lac Sam's keeper wound her leash around his forearm and dragged her forward. Again she stumbled and fell, sprawling before Hum Lo's table.

The Great Leader laughed, his fat body jiggling under his robe like a dough boy. "So, Ki Lim," he said, turning to face his second-in-command. "Here is the little plaything you requested. A gift to you, my brother, to amuse yourself with. Indeed, a reward for your excellent work on the unfortunate *Empress Christina*."

Hum Lo raised his wine goblet. Light glinted over the diamonds and sapphires of his ringed fingers. He smiled a big, toothy smile. "A toast to our brother Ki Lim for his great victory in the recent enterprise!"

Around the room the captains of the Red Vengeance cheered and raised their goblets in a toast.

"Bring her closer," Hum Lo commanded, beckoning toward Lac Sam with a curled index finger.

The young Vietnamese prisoner hung her head in shame, unable to bear the look of these men.

"Hold her head back. Show us her eyes," Hum Lo instructed.

The man holding the leash grabbed a handful of Lac Sam's hair and jerked her back, forcing her to look up into Hum Lo's jovial face.

He eyed her curiously.

"This is your new master, sweet thing," Hum Lo said, smiling. He gestured to the short, thin man beside him. Ki Lim looked like a leopard eyeing his prey. "I hope you enjoy him as much as he, I'm sure, will enjoy you!"

Lac Sam felt the hand clutching her hair loosening. She lowered her head once again, unable to bear the humiliation as the man's laughing eyes danced upon her naked body.

Abruptly Hum Lo's face darkened. He roared, "Show us the bitch's face!"

Lac Sam's keeper grabbed her collar in his fist and forced her head up again. The pressure around her neck closed off her breathing. Her eyes went wide as she gasped for air.

"Show everyone!" Hum Lo shouted.

Her captor twisted, turning Lac Sam slowly around the room. She clawed at her throat to loosen the collar, but to no avail. The assembled pirate captains' curiosity turned to astonishment and gasps of alarm. Some muttered and whispered to their neighbors. Two words, repeated among the men, reached Hum Lo's ears.

"Yes, brothers! Beware the evil eye! Our brother Ki Lim, it seems, wishes to live on the edge of great danger!"

Ki Lim rose quickly, suddenly worried at the effect Hum Lo's words were having on the assembled gathering.

"Brothers, do we not have protection against blue eyes?" Quickly he pulled up the long, wide sleeves of his robe, revealing large, spiraling tattoos on both arms. "Are we not all so marked to ward off evil?" He dropped his sleeves. He could see the men were listening to him.

"Besides—" He laughed and sneered, waving his arms toward Lac Sam. She was choking, her face turning red. Terrible scraping sounds came from her throat as she tried desperately to take in air. "Besides, her blue eyes give her no power. Look at her now!" Around the room some of the men began to laugh.

Hum Lo smiled at Ki Lim and raised his goblet again. "To pleasure!" he proposed. "And do not think that your Great Leader has forgotten any of you!"

Another rousing cheer, and the clinking of metal goblets filled the ship's mess as the captains toasted and drank. Lac Sam's keeper released the collar. She sank to her knees, sobbing and gasping for air.

Hum Lo put his arms up to call for silence. His voice grew low and serious.

"I am generous with my women slaves as you well know, but let no one here forget that, according to the customs of our ancient society, the Red Vengeance, the women are mine to distribute as I please. Yesterday two sailors of this ship forgot that. A woman who belonged to me was killed. The law of the Red Vengeance is sacrosanct. He who breaks our law will receive vengeance as red as the blood of our enemies!''

At the back of the hall a door opened, and Chung Hee slipped quietly inside. He moved quickly to the head table, where he whispered in Hum Lo's ear. The Red Vengeance leader nodded and waved him away.

Hum Lo swept his arms wide, crying to Lac Sam's keeper, ''Take her away! What follows, no one outside the Red Vengeance may see!''

The young girl felt the chain tightening. Ki Lim snapped his fingers. The collar jerked. She stood and was led quickly from the room.

''Oh, my brothers,'' Hum Lo continued. ''My faithful servant Chung Hee has brought news of a rich American yacht sailing across the China Sea, filled with money, equipment and women. The ship's name is *Diogenes*. And we will take it!''

Cheers exploded from the assembled pirates until Hum Lo raised his hands to quiet them.

''The executions of the two criminals will take place shortly, and their deaths will serve us in the secret ritual that is about to follow. The oracle has told me that the god of war rides in the sky at this very moment, and who can say what this fate will bring to us. Undoubtedly great riches and victories. You are my brothers, and I am your Great Leader. But I cannot serve forever.''

Cries and protests broke from the pirate captains. One man shouted, "Hum Lo will live forever," and his call was joined by the others.

The Red Vengeance leader put his hands up to quiet them. "Ki Lim has served me faithfully for many years. It has long been known that when my time passes he will be your next Great Leader. I ask all of you, now, to accept him as such, and we will seal our vows with the Ultimate Ritual, known only to the captains of the Red Vengeance."

For a moment Hum Lo's speech was broken by low whispers as the pirate captains rapidly consulted with one another. One of them stood and bowed low before the head table.

"Hum Lo, our Great Leader, has been stern but merciful. His charity is as great as his wrath. He rewards the righteous with women and gold and those who do wrong with the vengeance that is their blood. We accept his decision, and although we pray to the great heavens that it will be many decades before it comes to pass, should the Great Leader be called away, we shall be the servants of Ki Lim."

Hum Lo looked at the captains of the Red Vengeance. A little smile played on his lips. He chuckled. A laugh rolled through his great body, followed by another. He threw his head back and laughed strong and heartily. Slowly the other captains in the room began to laugh, too, one by one, until the room resounded with their mirth.

Hum Lo clapped his ringed hands and beckoned to the servants who stood waiting against the wall. "Bring in the prisoners, and we will seal our bargain!"

The doors at the back of the mess opened, and servers appeared, wheeling in two waist-high serving carts. The carts were carved from walnut and covered with ornately embroidered cloths. A domed silver lid rested on top of each cart.

They brought the carts to the center of the room, immediately in front of Hum Lo. The pirates were solemnly silent.

"It is a proverb of our ancestors that the man who does his work cheerfully shall never know want." Hum Lo beckoned to the servers.

The server by the first cart quickly lifted the silver cover. Hum Lo smiled.

Only the prisoner's head stuck out of a round hole in the top of the cart. It was completely immobilized by leather straps at the neck and chin, and a wire band circled it at the level of the eyebrows.

The Asian's face was white, his grin twisted into a grimace of horror. His head had been shaved, and a thin red line encircled it just above the metal band.

"It has always made me sad to see someone die, however necessary that death may be," Hum Lo sighed. "Even so, you have never wanted for gold or women. Ki Lim is different. Think of how you will all be rewarded. Death makes Ki Lim happy!"

"Sometimes it is a tragedy to allow someone to live," Ki Lim replied to the Great Leader with a slight bow of deference.

Hum Lo nodded to the server at the first cart.

The server carefully lifted the top of the man's skull from his head, exposing the living brain underneath. Hum Lo eyed it as someone would a rare and favored delicacy.

"To the eternal future of the Red Vengeance, we dedicate our lives," he cried. He reached forward with his spoon and gouged a chunk of the man's brains from the vessel of his cranium. The prisoner's head quivered and trembled against the confining straps; the whites of his eyes fluttered as synapses exploded.

"Wheel it on," Hum Lo commanded. "And bring me the next!"

As the ritual proceeded, Chung Hee leaned across the cushions until his mouth was close to Ki Lim's ear.

"Honorable Ki Lim," he whispered, "I have received more information than merely the story of a rich yacht sailing for Borneo."

Ki Lim turned to Chung Hee, his dark eyes glinting sharply. "And what is that, Chung Hee?"

"This man with the white hair and blue eyes you seek has been seen in Songkhla. One of our people was killed by a woman friend of his in the street near the harbor. She could only be a devil to have done such a thing. Later he was also seen in a tavern with the woman and a group of men. Five of them.''

"Excellent," Ki Lim muttered. He watched as the second prisoner was uncovered and the top of his head removed.

"I trust you will remember, Honorable Ki Lim, the favor of secrecy that I have done," Chung Hee whispered.

"I will remember," Ki Lim promised. "And remember this. I will have this white-haired man. And I will swear before you right now, Chung Hee, that before long it will be his brains that we will feast upon."

8

Geoff Bishop adjusted the cyclic between his legs, tilting the tip-path plane of the helicopter just enough to squeeze a few last klicks per hour cruising speed.

"Sure feels good to be behind the controls of a Huey again, Colonel."

Barrabas nodded from the copilot's seat. "Yeah, like old times. There's something about Hueys and Southeast Asia that goes together. Always will."

Below, round and smooth, lay the wide expanse of the China Sea. The rich blue sky was cloudless, and the bright Asian sun splashed a blinding swath of silver across the cerulean waters.

From time to time great schools of fish or jumping dolphins were visible below the surface of the clear water. Occasionally a pleasure yacht or freighter sailed smoothly toward port. They had spotted the *Diogenes,* which Barrabas and Hatton had recognized from its markings, several hundred kilometers off the coast of the Malaysian peninsula, heading south to Borneo.

Everything seemed quiet.

That was the main bitch. They were looking for pirates.

Ryder's word had been good. A day earlier the mercs had reported to a navy air base hangar in the southern suburbs of Songkhla, where the old U.S. Army Huey had been waiting for them. When the SOBs had arrived, workmen were spray-painting the Thai Royal Navy markings out and doing an engine check.

"They started refueling?" Barrabas asked.

"Nope," Ryder said, shaking his head.

"Good." Barrabas pulled out one of the long, thin cigars he occasionally enjoyed and lit it. "So where did this old critter come from?"

"When our government started the Vietnamization program in the early seventies, we sold off a lot of surplus to our allies in the region. This helicopter saw a lot of action," Ryder told him. He pointed to the scars in the fuselage where shrapnel and bullet holes had obviously been patched and covered over. "But it's a tough old bird."

"They don't make them like they used to," Barrabas commented.

"And they never made two alike as it was," Bishop added. "If a Huey's going to last, you know within a couple of months. This one looks like it's been through the wringer. If it's still flying now, it's probably got another decade left in it."

"You know choppers," Ryder said, nodding appreciatively. "I'll give you my personal word on this one. Cruise speed in excess of two hundred klicks or about a hundred and twenty-five miles an hour. Range is usually about four hundred kilometers, but this one's been modified to carry extra fuel for long-distance ocean cruises. You'll max anywhere between six hundred and eight hundred klicks, depending on your load."

"And those rotor blades are broader than normal, aren't they?" Bishop asked.

"That's right. This is one of the 214 series. It has a higher rated transmission, and the broad blades boost your maximum speed to over 250 kph."

Bishop whistled between his teeth. The statistics were impressive for an old chopper. "Any other fancy options?"

"A few odds and ends that might come in handy. FLIR—Forward Looking Infrared—for night capability, as well as new radar, and AQS-13B variable depth sonar."

"Not bad."

Ryder looked soberly at Bishop. "It means you'll be almost as well equipped as the pirates."

Barrabas clamped down hard on the cigar and spoke between his teeth. "And hardware. What about the hardware? You got TOW missile carriers on each side. Enough for eight of them. What else?"

"There's an M-60 machine gun mounted inside the fuselage," Ryder replied. "I've also got lots of additional rounds for the Colt Commandos you were issued for the *Empress Christina*. As well as concussion grenades and hand-held launchers."

"And the TOW missiles?" Barrabas asked again. Tube launched, optically tracked, wire guided—with that kind of accuracy, a speed of almost a kilometer a second and a range of four klicks, the antitank, armor-piercing projectiles were just what was needed to blow a pirate ship out of the water.

Commander Ryder scratched the side of his head and looked slightly embarrassed. "Well, I'm working on it. The United Nations insists that the antipiracy units of the Thai navy use unarmed aircraft in pursuing..."

"What in hell...?" Barrabas jerked the cigar from his mouth and angrily exhaled a long plume of smoke.

"I know, I know." Ryder put up his hands and made a calming gesture. "It's crazy. Their side of it is that they're afraid the refugees will get hit in the cross fire if the aircraft fired during an actual pirate raid. So all the international funding that comes— even from the American government—has strings attached. I've pulled some of those strings to get you guys the unofficial authorization for this covert action as well as the basic hardware, but I still have to deal with the big guys in the Royal Thai Navy."

The long and short of it was that the admirals behind their desks at Royal Thai HQ had become skittish and had ordered the TOWs removed from the chopper and replaced with the M-60. The latter was a great machine gun, but it reduced effective firing range to less than a kilometer—not the happiest margin in an air-sea attack. Commander Ryder was still trying to have the TOW released, however.

"Maybe for your second reconnaissance," he told Barrabas hopefully. "I'm doing everything I can."

Barrabas believed him.

Twenty-four hours later, the SOBs were cruising several thousand feet over the China Sea and coming up with zilch for their efforts.

In the fuselage, Lee Hatton, Claude Hayes, Nate Beck, Billy Two and Alex Nanos were dressed in full combat fatigues, with rappel harnesses strapped to their waists. The belt feed ran into the jaw of the M-60, and the rappel ropes for descending from the chopper onto the deck of a pirate boat were coiled and ready.

All they needed was pirates.

They did what every other soldier has done before battle. They waited.

Hayes stripped and cleaned one of the spare Commandos. Billy Two sat cross-legged with his eyes closed. Lee Hatton and Nate Beck stood by the door and surveyed the ocean below. Nanos sat off by himself, silent and contrite. Other than the occasional grunt of consent, Alex hadn't said a word to any of the other mercs since the evening in the tavern two days earlier.

Lee kept looking over at the Greek. Finally she left Nate by the door and walked over to Nanos. "Where's that old Alex humor," she asked, sitting down beside him. "I haven't heard a wisecrack in a while."

"I dunno," Alex replied without hesitation. "I think that old Alex humor realized what a jerk it had to deal with so it got up and left."

Lee nodded as if she'd just been convinced. "Probably a good move. Alex, what in hell is bugging you? For two days now you've been acting like Russia and the U.S. declared peace."

"This!" Alex said, turning his head up and pointing to the fading purplish bruise on the side of his chin. "Ah, I was a jerk. I deserved it."

Lee shrugged. "Listen, we'd just finished an assignment, and it didn't turn out the way any of us wanted it to. We all blow off steam in our own way. So you were drinking, you got a little out of line, and the colonel socked you to make you toe it."

Alex looked at her askance. "Having too much beer is a lousy excuse. I was just thinking with my balls instead of my brains."

"You've also had it in for Geoff Bishop ever since he came aboard, Alex. Why?"

Nanos leaned his head against the wall of the fuselage and looked off into space. "I dunno. Jealous, maybe. I knew you two were...doing it." He half laughed and winked at her.

Lee smiled in spite of herself. "Yeah. The big secret."

"I guess at first I wondered who he was. We all know you're a big girl and you can take care of yourself, Lee. But you know how guys are. Besides, I never had a little sister. It gave me a good feeling to...uh..."

"Be protective."

"That's it!"

"I like it, too. I never had any big brothers. But you're right. I am a big girl, and some decisions I can make for myself. You don't have to worry about Geoff."

"You like him a lot?" Alex asked.

Lee nodded quickly. "But I like you all a lot."

"I'm sorry for all the shit."

"Hey, Alex—" Lee put up her hands "—don't tell that to me. Tell it to the guy driving this helicopter."

In the cockpit of the Huey, Bishop pulled on the collective and skillfully fine-tuned the throttle manually to increase rpm. The chopper climbed higher into the atmosphere. The thinner air was cooler and drier. Since they were already flying through a high-pressure zone, it maximized lift and gave the chopper a slightly greater margin of speed in relation to gas consumption.

Bishop and Barrabas rode in silence for a long time, their eyes scanning the ocean, looking for anything remotely resembling the kind of big modern fishing trawler the pirates used.

"Have you and Alex talked yet?" Barrabas asked Bishop out of the blue. He surveyed the Canadian pilot with a sideways glance.

For a moment Bishop stared straight ahead, not answering. "About what?" he asked tightly.

"I figure I'd be angry, too," Barrabas said, nodding as if he agreed.

"Colonel, he's been on my case since day one. Like, what'd I do?" The pilot exhaled heavily with frustration and shook his head slowly. "I can't deal with it much longer, Colonel." He looked at Barrabas. "I really can't."

Barrabas was silent. It was his turn to stare out the window and think of how to handle the situation. Both Bishop and Nanos were good men, good fighters, and valuable on the team. But sometimes putting two guys together was like setting gelignite next to a bonfire, and there was nothing anyone could do about it until one or the other got shot and the problem took care of itself. That was the last thing Barrabas was going to let happen to the SOBs.

"You won't have to," Barrabas finally said. He changed the subject. "How's fuel?"

"We're almost half down, not including the re-serve," Bishop answered. "I'd say we have about ten minutes before we have to turn back. Unless you want to chew up the reserve and take a chance on healthy tail winds."

"Uh-uh. It's not worth it today. We haven't seen dick all. It's my guess the pirates aren't out there to-day. Our next reconnaissance is tonight. Maybe we'll have those TOWs by then to help us out. Take us home, Geoff, and we'll write this one off as a dry run."

DREW STEVENS STOOD at the door to the first state-room of the *Diogenes* and shouted to her father and fiancé on the bridge.

"Daddy, Kyle, I fixed us a late lunch. Why don't you leave the thing on automatic and come down to eat."

Ted Stevens, a tall, heavyset man with deeply tanned skin and graying sideburns, looked at his fu-ture son-in-law and shook his head with mock sad-ness. "Kids today..."

Kyle Carrington waved at Drew. The two tall, slender California blondes looked enough alike to be brother and sister. Everyone thought they were the perfect couple—a "matching set," people joked.

"Sure, honey, we'll do that. We'll be right down."

Drew blew him a kiss and disappeared below deck.

Kyle took off his sunglasses and picked up the snow-white tennis shirt draped over the wheel. "What do you mean, 'kids today,' Pops?" he asked with a friendly laugh. "We're both halfway through our twenties."

Stevens shook his head and acted indignant. "She says, 'Leave the thing on automatic.' The 'thing' she's talking about is my four-hundred-thousand-dollar fiberglass dream boat. And putting it on automatic misses the point of the whole adventure. Wind, sea and sun. Man struggling against the elements. Survival of the fittest!"

Ted Stevens took a deep breath and surveyed the endless blue expanse of the South China Sea. Except for a few fishing trawlers to the east, the *Diogenes* was completely alone.

"Thirty-five years as a corporate lawyer in San Francisco," he said, staring into the light wind blowing up from the Indian Ocean. "It finally paid off when I cashed in my chips after Betty died. It's been my dream since childhood to sail around the world."

"Well, Drew and I feel real privileged that you brought us along with you."

"Put the thing on automatic," Ted Stevens snorted. The sails were down, so he set the cruise control for the twin engines to a steady four knots. "I've never been happier," he said confidently.

"And I've rarely been hungrier," Kyle said, standing by the ladder leading to the main deck. The two men went below.

A little while later they had finished up the plate of thick ham sandwiches with hot Dijon mustard and potato salad.

"Look, I made you all my favorite dessert," Drew said, setting little glass bowls of fruit salad in front of the two men. "Those fishing boats out there are coming this way," she added, almost as an afterthought.

Ted Stevens and Kyle Carrington looked out the portholes. "Coming this way! They look like they're coming right at us!" Kyle said.

They'd been below deck for less than an hour, but in that time the fishing trawlers that had been dots on the horizon had moved speedily across the water. There were three of them, one quite large and two smaller, and they were less than half a kilometer off the port side.

"Wow! Look at the way the front of the big one is painted," Drew exclaimed. "Like a fire-breathing woman."

"Guess we'd better go up and say hello." Ted Stevens threw down his napkin and pushed himself up from the chair. He left the cabin.

"Are you coming, Kyle?" Drew asked as she headed after him.

Kyle hesitated. "Yeah, sure. In just a second." He waited until Drew left, then he pulled up the cushioned lid of the storage compartment behind the table and removed a semiautomatic rifle. He checked the clip and went on deck to join the welcoming party.

9

Ki Lim and Hum Lo watched from the bridge as the *Blood Maiden* swept toward the *Diogenes*. Two smaller trawlers sailed several hundred meters away, one on each side of the *Blood Maiden*.

"Cut the engines!" Hum Lo ordered. Another sailor spoke rapidly into the intercom to the engine room.

Hum Lo plucked the radio mouthpiece from its cradle and raised it close to his mouth.

"Maintain speed until you're past the yacht," he instructed the captains of the two smaller trawlers.

Ki Lim quietly raised a set of powerful binoculars to his eyes and brought them into focus.

The name of the yacht, *Diogenes*, was painted on the bow, and an American flag rippled at the stern. A middle-aged man with graying hair emerged from the stateroom. He was unarmed. Walking to the side of the yacht, he stared curiously across the water separating the *Diogenes* from the *Blood Maiden*, then he raised his arm and waved.

Ki Lim lowered the binoculars, an insistent smile playing across his lips.

"There will not be any resistance, Great Leader," he said. "It appears they think this is a friendly call. The yacht is American. Americans are so naive. Innocent. Like children."

"Reverse engines!" Hum Lo shouted to the crew. Again a sailor quickly repeated the order into the intercom. Hum Lo reached for the binoculars. "Let me see," he said. He searched the deck of the *Diogenes*. Two more people emerged from the stateroom and joined the older man on the deck. Both were blond. One was a woman.

"We have a rare fish before us, brother," Hum Lo said enigmatically, curling his bushy eyebrows. He invited Ki Lim to look through the binoculars again.

"A blond woman. How wonderful!" Ki Lim exclaimed. "But, Great Leader, you realize that in all likelihood she will have blue eyes, too."

Hum Lo smiled. "But she has yellow hair, not black like the whore you have taken. It's not the same. This one will be my pleasure, and mine alone."

"It is as you wish, Great Leader." Ki Lim bowed slightly to Hum Lo. "A great victory deserves great rewards."

Hum Lo nodded with satisfaction and moved toward the door. "I will board this yacht personally with the men of the Red Vengeance. Will you join me, brother?"

Ki Lim took one last lingering look through the binoculars at the beautiful woman on the American yacht. He wanted her for his collection.

He vowed to have her.

TED AND DREW STEVENS watched from the deck of the *Diogenes* as the bow of the *Blood Maiden* loomed above them, several dozen meters away.

"My God, look at the design painted on the bow of that ship!" Ted exclaimed. "It's incredible. I've never seen anything like it. It'd be worth a fortune in San Francisco."

The face and upper torso of a bare-breasted woman flowed back along each side of the hull of the *Blood Maiden*, coming together at the bow. She had great red eyes and spewed fire as if it were a waterfall of blood. Her black hair was swept back, and painted into it were long streamers of seaweed and small shark-toothed fish.

Drew nodded. "It is beautiful," she said less enthusiastically, "if a little macabre. It must be some kind of sea goddess or something."

Kyle Carrington stood back slightly from the side of the yacht without commenting. He'd left the semiautomatic rifle just behind the door to the stateroom where it was hidden from sight but easily accessible. There was something strange about this encounter in the middle of the China Sea; it didn't feel right.

The two smaller fishing boats that had gone past had stopped and reversed to face the *Diogenes* at the bow and at the stern. The big trawler was aimed straight at the middle of the luxury yacht. The *Diogenes* was now the center of a triangle with a ship at each corner. High on the bow of the big trawler, sailors ran quickly back and forth, their jabbering shouts audible to the Americans on the yacht.

Suddenly an Asian man, holding a loudspeaker, appeared at the tip of the *Blood Maiden*'s bow.

"Hi there!" Ted Stevens shouted, waving his arm. "How y'all doing?"

Two other sailors near the man with the loudspeaker drew the canvas cover from a piece of bulky equipment.

It was a machine gun.

Without a moment's hesitation, one of the sailors lowered the barrel. Light yellow muzzle flash popped, and bullets pounded into the side of the *Diogenes*.

Drew screamed. Her father jumped back from the side, tripping and falling. Kyle shot forward and threw his body around Drew to cover her.

Splinters of paint, wood and fiberglass exploded into the breeze and settled on the water, floating.

The machine-gun fire was brief.

Immediately the man with the loudspeaker spoke up, in English with a rounded Asian accent.

"Raise hands into air. Now. Or we will kill."

The barrel of the machine gun turned lazily back to center on the three Americans. The Stevenses and Kyle Carrington were frozen in shock. The machine gun exploded again. More hot lead chewed into the wooden deck, throwing splinters against their legs.

"Now!" the man screamed at them through the loudspeaker.

Slowly Ted Stevens rose to his feet. Drew and Kyle pulled apart. They raised their hands in the air. Drew sobbed with terror. Ted Stevens's face had drained of color.

"You will stand without moving until further notice!" the amplified voice from the trawler told them.

It seemed to them that they stood that way for hours under the heavy eye of the machine gun. Then the motor launches, filled with heavily armed men, were lowered from the side of the trawler.

The boats came alongside the yacht, and the pirates climbed over the edge, clutching their automatic rifles.

The short, wiry Asians were a terrifying bunch. They wore light khaki pants and shirts of Western style, but their sun-bronzed arms and necks were covered with elaborate tattoos of strange spirals and many-headed, half-human monsters. Their biceps were ringed with silver armlets, and golden chains hung around their necks. Their ears and nipples were pierced by little gold rings, and many of them wore brightly colored bandannas tied around their heads to cover their hair.

They looked like pirates who had leaped two hundred years through history. But the assortment of pistols, new and old automatic rifles, the belts of mags and ammunition, the small portable radio transmitters attached to the belts at their waists made it clear that these pirates had entered the twentieth century.

They swarmed over the sides of the *Diogenes* and quickly surrounded the prisoners. To one side, at the stern, some of the pirates helped an enormously fat man from the motor launch onto the yacht. He wore a coat of red and gold brocade, and his rings were studded with precious and semiprecious stones. He glanced quickly, almost disinterestedly, at the Americans as he heaved his great body aboard.

He was followed by a short, wiry Asian dressed in tight black pants and shirt. This one had dark eyes that glinted like polished Alaskan diamonds, and a thin, carefully trimmed mustache accentuated the lines of his cruel mouth. His hand rested on the hilt of a long, curved machete, belted to his side with a broad, colorful woven belt.

Kyle watched carefully the movement of the pirates. They strode slowly around the deck of the *Diogenes*, examining equipment and keeping their eyes on the prisoners. So far none of them had gone below, and he assumed they were waiting for instructions from their leaders.

Hum Lo and Ki Lim walked forward to where the prisoners stood with their hands raised, looking them over like pieces of meat hanging in a butcher's shop. The big one began to chuckle, and he talked to the other one in their Asian tongue.

With their leaders present, the other pirates had relaxed and taken their eyes off the prisoners. Their backs were to the cabin door, and Kyle had a clear run to the automatic rifle. But what then? he thought. The moment he went for the gun, the pirates would mow down Ted and Drew Stevens. All he could do was wait.

Drew looked at her fiancé. She too remembered the gun below. But Ted Stevens was slipping into shock. His eyes had gone vacant with fear, and his face had drained completely of color. Stevens had a heart condition.

Kyle prayed silently for luck.

For a miracle.

THE WINDS HAD CHANGED DIRECTION, slowing the Huey as the SOBs headed back to Songkhla.

"It's going to be tighter than I thought, fuelwise," Bishop told Barrabas.

"But we'll make it?" the white-haired colonel asked speculatively.

"Oh, yeah. We'll make it with most of the reserve tank left. But when you're in an aircraft, and there's no place to go but down, that's tight."

"Seems to me you've been in this situation before," Barrabas said as he smiled.

Bishop laughed at the memory the colonel alluded to. After his military career in the Canadian air force, Bishop had flown commercial jets. One day, on a flight out of Vancouver, someone had made an error in refueling. He was halfway across the prairies with two hundred and fifty passengers when he had run out of gas. He had brought the jet down on a long, straight stretch of Trans-Canada Highway just outside of Winnipeg. The only casualty was a traveling salesman who didn't get out of the way in time. As a reward for saving the lives of his passengers and crew, the airline company had suspended Bishop. The whole incident had created a stir, particularly when the pilots' association had turned around and given him an award. That was how Barrabas had found out about him. Bishop had been down on his luck, spewn out of the system by its own sheer inanity—just like most of the mercs had been before they were recruited. Nile Barrabas had offered him a job. The occupational hazards of being a merc were high, but so were the rewards.

Barrabas raised the binoculars and stared intently at the ocean far ahead.

"Pay dirt," he muttered. "Eleven o'clock, check it out."

Bishop squinted to bring the tiny black shapes into focus. "Ships?"

"A boarding party. There's a big fishing trawler and two smaller fishing boats congregating in the general area of a sixty-foot yacht." Barrabas turned around and yelled into the fuselage. "Dr. Hatton! Up front on the double. The rest of you are on alert."

A moment later Lee poked her head into the cockpit. Barrabas handed her the binoculars and pointed. "Tell me if you recognize that yacht."

Hatton studied the vessels for a moment. They were a long way off, but the long, sleek lines of Stevens's boat were unmistakable.

"The *Diogenes*," she said, keeping the binoculars to her eyes. The gaudy painting of the fire-breathing mermaid on the front of the trawler was coming into focus. "That other ship, whatever it is, it's... wait a second. That ain't no ordinary fishing trawler, Colonel. Not unless they shoot the fish from the bow with a machine gun."

She passed the glasses back to Barrabas.

"How fast can we get there, Geoff?" Barrabas asked the pilot.

"Ten minutes." Bishop reached for the cyclic to turn the chopper. His eyes wandered uneasily to the fuel gauge.

Barrabas unstrapped his seat belt and leaned into the fuselage. "Battle stations, everyone. There's a pirate boarding party in progress, and we're going to gate-crash."

ON THE DIOGENES Ted Stevens had recovered sufficiently to deal with the pirates American style.

"I have money here. I'll give you money if you just leave us alone."

Hum Lo smiled, and his body shook, slowly at first. Then he erupted into laughter, and the flesh of his jowls and his belly jiggled like jelly. "Ha, ha...Ki Lim, he is offering us his money. Ha, ha!"

Ki Lim returned Hum Lo's look and chuckled.

The pirate leader turned back to Ted Stevens, his voice deadly serious. "Where is it?"

"Down below! It's hidden, in a secret..."

"Father!"

"Mr. Stev...!"

Drew and Kyle both exclaimed simultaneously. A pirate slammed the butt of his automatic rifle into Carrington's kidney. The young man groaned sharply, then stifled it. He bent over as the agony swept through him.

"Twenty thousand dollars!" Stevens said in a rush. "It's hidden behind a panel over the dining table, below deck."

"Get it," Hum Lo said curtly to his men. Three of them immediately went below deck. The sounds of rifles smashing and splintering the expensive wood paneling reverberated through the yacht.

"Search everything!" Hum Lo shouted to the pirates who were still above deck. "Strip it! Take everything valuable!"

The pirates of the Red Vengeance leaped into action. There was a din of breaking glass and furniture, and soon a steady stream of pirates emerged from below deck carrying away clothing, furniture, bottles of liquor, the television, radio, camera equipment, kitchen utensils, fishing gear, scuba equipment, the VCR, a video movie collection, a carved ivory chess set, the stereo and the navigational equipment—everything except the automatic rifle, which still appeared to be hidden safely behind the door to the first cabin.

Other pirates with greasy tools swarmed over the deck, stripping the riggings, the engines and the bridge of everything movable.

Ted Stevens stood there, helplessly witnessing the destruction of his dream, tears streaming down his face and into his open mouth.

Ki Lim went below deck to supervise the stripping of the *Diogenes*. Hum Lo's men had managed to destroy almost an entire wall of the stateroom without finding the hidden money.

"Over the table!" he yelled at them, motioning to the other side of the room where the dining table was hinged to the wall. A sailor brought his rifle down across the table. It collapsed. They started smashing the wood paneling with their rifles.

Ki Lim beckoned to one of the sailors. The little man scurried over and gave a little bow of his head. Ki Lim slipped a limpet mine from the inner folds of his jacket.

"Put this on the fuel tanks," he instructed the sailor.

"As you wish, great sir." The pirate took the explosive device and quickly bowed again. He obediently ran off to do Ki Lim's bidding. The other pirates had smashed through into the secret compartment and had found an aluminum briefcase with a combination lock. "Take it on deck!" Ki Lim ordered.

He followed.

The two pirates from below presented the briefcase to Hum Lo.

"Open it!" the Great Leader ordered Stevens.

The middle-aged man stumbled forward and fumbled with the twin combination locks. It took him several attempts in his nervousness. Finally the case opened, revealing crisp rows of smooth, neat American bills.

Hum Lo's eyes lit up.

"Please. Take it. Take all of it," Stevens begged. "Just leave us alone."

The *Blood Maiden* had pulled in right beside the *Diogenes*, and the hydraulic winches had been swung over the yacht. Pirate sailors pulled on the wire cables, and the machinery began to hum. Stevens's mouth dropped as his twin turbo engines rose from their compartments.

"Noooo! Please, not..."

"Shut up, old man!" Hum Lo said with annoyance.

"You bastards." Kyle tried to jump forward in his anger. "You've already taken the sails..." A sailor moved quickly in front of him and pushed him back with his rifle.

Hum Lo eyed Drew and took a couple of steps forward until he was standing in front of her.

"Such a pretty thing," he said in a singsong voice, bending his head to search her face. Drew stared back defiantly, then looked away.

"And she hates me, too," Hum Lo said. He sounded as if it was too bad. "Well, maybe we can do something about that," he taunted her. He raised his arm and caressed her breast with his index finger. Drew caught her breath, trembling to hold back her fear and anger as he felt her over like a piece of meat.

Kyle moved forward, but his way was blocked by the mean-looking pirate with the automatic rifle.

Ted Stevens turned white again and gasped for air. He groaned and clutched his chest, his eyes rolling up into his head.

"Daddy!" Drew shrieked.

She threw herself toward her father as he collapsed to his knees. He tugged blindly at his chest, where the veins and arteries of his heart had blown apart like a frayed garden hose.

Hum Lo reached out and grabbed Drew with his big, powerful arm. He pulled her to him and squeezed her against his fat body as she struggled to reach her dying father.

Ki Lim watched with a slight smile as Stevens keeled over backward, groaning and quivering as life left his body.

Drew shrieked and screamed hysterically, struggling against Hum Lo's arm.

"Let him die," Ki Lim said, nodding to Stevens.

"Of course," Hum Lo said comfortably. He moved his arm to Drew's neck, his big hand squeezing her throat and choking off half her air. Then he threw her to one of his sailors.

"Take her aboard the *Blood Maiden*. Chain her and put her in my quarters. No! Better yet, throw her in with the other women. She must begin to learn that she is a whore!"

Drew screamed and kicked as the sailor moved in, grabbing her arms and twisting them behind her.

All was chaos aboard the *Diogenes*. The winches whined as the engines were lifted into the air. The pirates shouted and boasted as they loaded their loot into large cargo nets that had been dropped from the

Blood Maiden. Then there was another sound, hardly audible at first.

An aircraft motor. Coming closer.

Ki Lim heard it.

He looked up, trying to zero in on what it was and where it was coming from. Hum Lo and the other pirates heard it, too. They stopped and listened intently.

Kyle Carrington saw his chance. He stepped back and made a run for the automatic rifle.

10

"Our luck's holding!" Barrabas said, observing the pirate ship and the *Diogenes* through his field glasses as the chopper approached at full speed. They were almost on top of the pirates, and they hadn't been noticed.

The two smaller fishing boats had sailed off, leaving the big trawler with the painted bow alone with the yacht. The *Blood Maiden* had sailed up beside the *Diogenes*, and the colonel could see its winches lifting the yacht's engines aboard. Armed pirates carrying booty were swarming across the deck of the luxury boat, but the cabin housing partially obscured the leaders and the prisoners.

And there was still the M-60 on the bow of the trawler to worry about.

"Take a run over the pirate ship so we can knock out the machine guns and any other mounted hardware first," Barrabas told Bishop. He turned around and shouted to the mercs in the fuselage. "Alex, Billy and Lee, break out the M-79s. I want one up here, too."

The mercs had opened the long doors in the side of the chopper. Claude Hayes and Nate Beck took charge of the M-60, with Claude aiming and Nate ready to feed the disintegrating link belt of standard NATO 7.62 mm rounds.

Nanos and Starfoot checked the rappel rigging on the floor of the Huey. Three ropes were wound to inset triangulated bolts. The ropes had been coiled accordion style and secured with elastic retaining bands. The running end of each rope was weighted with a sandbag, and the whole assembly had been inserted into rucksacks that lay near the open side. The edge of the Huey had been padded to eliminate friction and fraying when the rucksacks were kicked out and the ropes were down.

"Looks good, Billy Two!" Nanos crowed. He threw the Osage and Lee Hatton separate coiled lengths of rope, which they began wrapping around themselves in Swiss seats.

Lee reached through the doorway to the cockpit, handing the colonel the M-79 grenade launcher, grenade cartridges and some spare mags of 5.56 for his Colt Commando.

"I want you, Billy and Nanos to drop as many grenades as we can on the deck of the trawler when Bishop flies over, while Claude and Nate cover with the M-60. When we fly over the yacht, you can give backup with your autorifles," Barrabas told Hatton. "But watch out for the owners of the yacht. If they're alive and on deck, they'll be in our firing lines.''

Barrabas broke the M-79 open, released the safety and pushed the grenade cartridge in until the rim of the case hit the extractor. He closed the snub-nosed weapon and checked the sights. The M-79 was an ugly thing, resembling a sawed-off shotgun, and with developments of integral grenade launchers for combat rifles, it was almost obsolete. But it was lightweight, highly accurate and had a range of up to half a kilometer. That gave the pirates a half-klick advantage with the machine gun on the bow of their ship. But rifle attachments wouldn't help the mercs out any better than the M-79. Barrabas cursed the absence of the TOW missiles once again. It was always comforting to even out the odds when going into battle. For the SOBs the odds were rarely even.

''Give me first crack on the gun at the bow,'' Barrabas told Bishop. He released his seat belt and stuck the snub-nosed launcher out the window.

Bishop twisted the cyclic pitch control, and the Huey veered sideways, doing a high-speed cruise that brought it around facing the bows of the two vessels.

Pirates ran back and forth along the decks, scaling rope ladders that led from the yacht to the trawler. Barrabas could see the prisoners finally, surrounded by a small circle of armed pirates. One man was supine on the deck, dead or wounded. Two of the pirates had seized a second prisoner, and it looked like it was the woman. The third one turned to the cabin door as other pirates ran to the bow of the *Diogenes*. Small orange flashes sparked on the deck.

"They just saw us!" Barrabas shouted.

The first flak sounds outside the chopper confirmed it.

"Open up, Hayes!" Barrabas ordered. "Hit the hull of the trawler where they're climbing!"

The M-60 replied at six hundred rounds a minute. Cartridge casings did their happy dance into the air as Nate fed the gun. They bounced on the floor of the Huey and rolled downhill into space. Bishop veered sharply over the ship, bringing them into range.

Three of the pirates scaling the ropes on the hull dropped suddenly into the water.

On the deck of the *Blood Maiden*, the crew forgot about the *Diogenes*'s diesel engines and left them swinging in midair. They ran for the machine gun at the bow and to the second one on the bridge.

The barrels swung at the chopper and spat orange kisses.

"Jesus," Bishop muttered as tracers streaked around the glass bubble of the cockpit.

The sound of the bullets chunking into the underbelly of the Huey was like a punch in the stomach. For all of them.

ON THE DIOGENES Kyle Carrington slipped inside the door to the stateroom just as the first burst of machine-gun fire exploded against the hull of the *Blood Maiden*.

"Get him!" Hum Lo roared, his face red and suddenly sweaty. "Shoot that down!" He pointed to the helicopter.

Three of his sailors, climbing the rope ladders that led to the deck of the *Blood Maiden*, sprouted big red polka dots on their backs. Their brief screams were choked off as they fell. Two disappeared into the narrow crack between the two boats and splashed into the water. The third thudded onto the railing around the deck of the *Diogenes*. Pirates ran for the bow of the yacht, holding their automatic rifles up to fire at the helicopter, which came in lower and headed for the bow of the *Blood Maiden*. The sudden chatter of machine-gun fire from the bow and bridge of the trawler told Hum Lo that the Red Vengeance was fighting back.

Drew Stevens screamed and twisted, suddenly breaking away from the Great Leader.

The helicopter dodged from side to side, successfully avoiding the pirates' return fire.

Ki Lim drew his machete as lead from the chopper's M-60 pounded into the *Diogenes*. The pirates dived for cover.

BISHOP TILTED THE HUEY, giving Barrabas a clear forty-five-degree angle from his grenade launcher to the machine gun on the bow of the *Blood Maiden*. His arms pulled and his hands twisted from throttle to collective to cyclic control as he bounced the chopper from side to side, up and down, zigzagging it in three dimensions across the water.

On the bow of the *Blood Maiden*, pirate sailors worked feverishly to aim the two machine guns at the erratic Huey. A steady stream of orange streaks whizzed around the cockpit.

Barrabas positioned himself as best he could by crouching in the seat and keeping his elbow and arm off the window of the chopper. He aimed down the sights of the M-79, steadied momentarily and squeezed the trigger.

The grenade exploded on impact.

The pirates congregating at the bow gun vaporized in a cloud of smoke, fire, shrapnel, limbs, bone and bits of useless ordnance.

One down.

The second machine gun on the bridge swung around to stare at the cockpit as Bishop raced the chopper over the deck of the trawler.

Bullets splayed into metal just above their heads, too close to the delicate and vital rotor mechanism for comfort.

"Whooooeeeee!" Bishop whooped. "Hang on!"

He turned the throttle to full gas and dived.

In the fuselage, meanwhile, Hayes had a clean view straight down onto the deck of the *Diogenes*. He could clearly see one man lying on the deck and the pirates struggling with a prisoner near the cabin door midship.

He tilted the M-60 until it was veering straight down, almost perpendicular to its mount. He laid a solid line of deadly lead across the yacht's deck, steering clear of the prisoners. The pirates who had momentarily swarmed across the boat, shooting at the Huey with their automatic rifles, quickly disappeared behind the cabin housing.

Nanos and Billy Two positioned themselves at the opposite door with M-79s.

"Strike one!" Nanos shouted when the machine gun at the bow was blown up by Barrabas's grenade.

"Strike two coming up," Billy Two muttered, sighting at the gun on the bridge. He squeezed.

The grenade left the M-79 with a hiss and a smoky tail as it sailed down.

Nanos fired immediately, and twin explosions ripped across the bridge of the *Blood Maiden*. The second gun blew into a cloud of spare parts, tossing pirates to the fish.

Automatic weapon fire opened up from all sides of the big boat.

"Here boys." It was Hatton. She handed each of them a loaded M-79 launcher, and they threw the empty ones down and grabbed the refreshments. She came to the door beside them, kneeling against the Huey's wall.

The three mercs fired almost in unison. More explosions tore across the stern of the *Blood Maiden*, reducing the surface fire by fifty percent. The trawler was fading quickly out of range.

The chopper tilted suddenly, throwing them back into the middle of the fuselage as Bishop spun the Huey around for a second run.

KYLE CARRINGTON STOOD INSIDE the ransacked stateroom and gazed straight into the eyes of one of Hum Lo's finest. Outside, the sounds of explosions and automatic rifle fire rocked the boat.

The short black-haired pirate looked up from the leather chair he was cutting to pieces and smiled at the escaping prisoner. The smile consisted of one gold tooth and two small yellowed ones. The rest was just gums.

He gave a kind of goofy laugh and brandished the knife. He looked Kyle over, laughed again and walked toward him. Kyle swallowed. It was quite clear what the pirate planned on using the knife for.

The American walked backward slowly with one hand out. With the other, he swung the inner door of the stateroom shut.

The pirate smiled his nearly toothless smile and slashed at the air with his long, sharp knife. It swished past Kyle, and the pirate laughed again.

Kyle took one more step back. His hand closed around the barrel of the rifle. He tightened his grip, moved quickly to one side and swung the butt of the rifle at the pirate's head. The butt impacted solidly with the pirate's skull, shattering the bone in a long, straight indentation from temple to crown. The two men stood frozen for a moment.

Then, as if on cue, blood shot from the pirate's mouth, nose, eyes and ears, spurting and splashing onto his tattooed naked arms and chest. His hand tightened on his knife for the last time. He keeled over backward and slumped to the floor.

Kyle turned the rifle around, jamming the bloody butt under his arm and against his chest. He ran from the stateroom onto the deck.

The explosions and autofire had died, and the drone of the helicopter was fading as it disappeared over the stern of the *Blood Maiden*.

Drew and Hum Lo lay sprawled on the deck. Drew screamed and struggled, trying to crawl away from the Great Leader. He held her ankle in one hand as he tried to raise himself to his feet. With an amazing agility for a man who weighed in at over three hundred pounds, he crawled forward and grabbed Drew by her belt. He stumbled to his feet, pulling her up with him. Then he raised his arm and struck her. His big hand flattened across her face.

She sank in his arms like a rag doll.

Kyle Carrington burst out of the door of the stateroom, flourishing the automatic rifle. He swung it to his shoulder and aimed for the Great Leader's wide forehead.

"Drop her, you bastard, or I'll blow your fucking brains out!"

Hum Lo froze and looked at Carrington. He didn't drop her. He held her unconscious body in front of him as a shield. His eyes drifted slowly back.

Ki Lim moved silently into the open behind Carrington. He held his machete up.

"Tricky bastard," Kyle muttered. "Drop her now!" he roared. His finger tightened on the trigger.

Hum Lo waited confidently for Ki Lim to strike.

Ki Lim didn't move. He stared back at the Great Leader.

"Kill himmm!" Hum Lo screamed, his face reddening even more and his eyes large with fury. It slowly dawned on him that he was about to be betrayed.

Ki Lim met his eyes and shook his head.

Hum Lo's mouth fell open. His face flooded purple, and thick veins ballooned along his forehead.

Carrington fired.

A small red hole blossomed in the center of Hum Lo's forehead. The back of his skull blew off in a shower of gray brain matter. Blood jetted forward, splashing Carrington and dribbling down Drew's unconscious body. The pirate leader's grip relaxed for the last time, and Drew slumped to the bloody deck.

Ki Lim struck. He sprang sideways, landing with both feet and bringing his machete down.

The blade severed Carrington's left arm at the wrist and cracked against the metal barrel of the rifle. The gun, with the hand still clinging to it, fell to the deck.

Carrington screamed, his body lurching suddenly into shock. He grabbed the blood-pumping stump of his arm and held it to staunch the flow.

Other pirates ran to the gory scene. Ki Lim shouted orders.

"Use the winch! I want these prisoners." He pointed to the cargo net lying on the forward deck, half filled with booty from the *Diogenes*. "Hurry! Quickly!"

Sailors carried Drew and threw her unconscious body into the net.

"Him, too!" Ki Lim shouted, pointing to Carrington, who stood quivering by the cabin door like a trapped and bloodied animal. "I do not want him to die! Not yet."

Ted Stevens still lay on the deck of the *Diogenes*. His skin was blue. He was dead. Too bad, thought Ki Lim. With a strong, swift stroke, he brought his machete down again and beheaded the corpse. He grabbed the head and tossed it into the cargo net like a basketball.

The helicopter was coming in for a second run at them. Ki Lim didn't have to look; he could hear it coming. Another cable with a heavy iron hook was lowered from the trawler's winch to the *Diogenes*. Ki Lim grabbed it. Quickly it pulled him up to the deck of the *Blood Maiden*.

BISHOP SWERVED THE HUEY steeply in a tight turn.

"Take it alongside the trawler where it faces the yacht," Barrabas told him. "We'll run some fire down that side and try to separate the two boats."

"Colonel, I hate to tell you this..." Bishop said reluctantly as the chopper swung around and started the cruise back. "We're not going to make it back to Songkhla unless we go now. Not enough gas."

"Goddamn, Bishop. We can get back to shore somewhere, can't we?"

"The Thai coast near Songkhla is the nearest dry land for a hundred kilometers."

"Does this thing float?"

Bishop shrugged. "Might. For a while."

"Then we have two choices. We float. Or we take those ships and ditch the chopper."

"Aye, aye, Colonel." Bishop twisted the throttle and leaned the Huey into a forward-attack angle.

"Forget the yacht for now. Let's go straight down the center of the trawler and we'll stop everything that moves."

Barrabas moved from the copilot's seat and went back to the fuselage. "Alex, Billy—stay on the grenades. You're doing a great job. We're going straight down the middle of the trawler. I want streams of fire coming out of each side of this chopper. Claude and Nate, keep down anything that moves with the M-60. Lee, you and I will cover with the Commandos where needed."

Lee Hatton was on her stomach on the floor of the Huey with her head stretched out the door and a pair of binoculars in front of her.

"Colonel, I don't like it. The pirates have retreated to the trawler. They winched up a pile of stuff, and now they're pulling away. There's no sign of life aboard the *Diogenes*."

Barrabas flattened himself beside her and took the field glasses.

The *Blood Maiden* was cutting through the water, leaving the *Diogenes* lifeless in its wake. The deck was red with blood and a body lay sprawled near the cabin. On the trawler a winch spun its cable, dropping a huge cargo net into one of the holds. Pirates rushed to take up positions along the deck.

Barrabas saw something that sent shudders up his spine.

"Holy shit." He scrambled away from the edge. Some of the pirates were carrying portable missile launchers. Very modern. Perhaps even heat sensitive.

If they were, it was curtains for the Huey.

"Back off, Bishop!" he shouted. His voice left no doubt in Bishop's mind that it was urgent. The mercs felt their stomachs crawl up to their mouths and dive back down again as the helicopter turned almost ninety degrees and spun backward.

Barrabas forced himself to the edge of the Huey and raised the field glasses again.

One of the pirates kneeled on the deck of the *Blood Maiden* and aimed the long tube over his shoulder. A short puff of smoke blew from the barrel.

Suddenly the *Diogenes* erupted like a volcano into a swirl of orange fire and debris, halfway between the Huey and the *Blood Maiden*. The concussion from the explosion swept back, rocking the helicopter.

Almost simultaneously a second explosion blossomed out from the center of the first one, sending sheets of water high in the air.

The explosion on the yacht had inadvertently decoyed the heat-sensitive missile.

The death of the *Diogenes* had saved them.

Barrabas pushed himself back from the edge of the fuselage door and shouted to the cockpit, ''Bishop, get us home before we run out of gas!''

''Looks like the Red Vengeance did it again,'' Claude Hayes said, standing back from the M-60 and looking around at the other mercs. Their faces and combat fatigues were stained with sweat, gun grease and black powder. Hundreds of cartridge casings rolled noisily across the floor. They looked at one another silently in the aftermath of the battle, concentrating on catching their breath.

There was nothing to say.

Visitors zero, home team two.

Barrabas made his way slowly to the front of the Huey. Now the SOBs had more to avenge besides the dead hostages of the *Empress Christina* and the poor young refugee girls who had been viciously raped as they made their escape to freedom.

He turned before entering the cockpit.

''We'll be back,'' he said solemnly. He swore.

11

For a week the mercs made runs across the China Sea from their base in Songkhla. Barrabas shifted the timing, giving them an equal number of night and evening runs. On the third run they came across a small flotilla of refugee boats drifting aimlessly, their sails stripped from the masts and their engines useless. The pirates had been there two days earlier.

They dropped water, fuel and medicine. Lee Hatton and Claude Hayes rappelled into the larger of the five boats and began treating some of the sick and wounded. Five hours later the Thai navy got there, and the refugees were taken aboard.

It was the same story once again. They'd been attacked and robbed. All the young women had been taken, the resisters had been killed and the survivors had drifted without food, fuel or water under the deadly sun of the China Sea for two days.

"The children died first," Lee said later. "Then the older ones. But even the fittest were on the verge of cannibalism by the time we got there."

Hayes shook his head long and slow in agreement. "Unh-huh. My feet touched the bottom of the boat. After I unhooked the ropes and you guys drove off, I turned around and saw the look in those poor people's eyes. I knew they was either going to greet us or eat us."

The SOBs continued daily runs. The schedule was hard. Six hours of cruising. Eight hours of rest. Six more hours of cruising. They saw the China Sea in many moods—with the sun rising and the sun setting, gray with torrential rains, or as blue as a swimming pool. They felt the heat burn up from it under the midday sun like a laser reflected from a mirror. And they felt the plunging night temperatures when the air became heavy with a deep, moist chill that shook the bones.

But they didn't see pirates.

It was hard as hell on the team. Ground time was limited, barely long enough to rest. And the chopper runs were long monotonous surveillance routines, with a rotating duty roster.

Twice Barrabas had come close to the Red Vengeance. Twice it had blown up in his face. During the surveillance runs, his eyes strained until they were bloodshot from searching the shiny water below. The pirates' absence was their presence, taunting him, challenging him, defying him.

There had to be a base somewhere, a port where the great trawler with the painted bow took on stores and was maintained. Thai navy intelligence had reports on a number of fishing villages scattered among the islands along the coasts of Thailand and Kampuchea where pirate ships were known to make regularly scheduled stops. But Barrabas knew from his examination of the information that none of the villages was big enough, or close enough to commercial supply routes, to serve as a major base.

He had no doubts that his soldiers could go on indefinitely the way they were. But they needed a break, something substantial. The pace was draining, and the lack of action so numbing that he was forced to watch morale plummet as the SOBs sank into silent defeat.

Barrabas needed two things: the location of the Red Vengeance's base and TOW missiles.

A week after the loss of the *Diogenes*, the colonel sat in a hard wooden chair in an office of the Royal Thai Navy's Regional Division Office. It was a dull, shabby high-ceilinged room. A long fluorescent light floated overhead, its stale gases quivering. Electricity crackled, and it threw almost imperceptibly thickening shadows across the dingy walls.

Commander Ryder sat on the other side of the big old desk. A bottle of Scotch and two glasses sat on the scarred wooden top. Ryder filled the glasses and handed one to Barrabas.

The colonel threw it back, his one and only finger of the day. The sudden fiery warmth in his stomach eliminated half the tension he had brought with him from the chopper. He set the empty glass down, rocked backward on the two rear legs of the chair and put his hands behind his head and one foot on the edge of the desktop.

"We need those TOWs, Lee."

Ryder jerked his tie loose and unbuttoned the collar of his military shirt.

"Sure feels good to get out of this monkey suit at the end of the day," he said. "I envy you, Nile. You were spared the fate that I succumbed to. There are rewards for staying on the inside, but there are punishments, too."

"It's handy to have friends, though." Barrabas looked directly at Ryder.

"Nile, it's not just a matter of TOW missiles and whether or not I can get them released for this covert action. It's a question now of whether this covert action will continue."

Barrabas dropped the chair forward with a crash. He straddled the seat and leaned toward Ryder with his elbows on the desk. "What do you mean?"

Ryder moved his shoulders uncomfortably and shifted down in his chair. "The Royal Thai General Staff had to approve it. Not the full General Staff, A smaller group of officers who believe firm action is necessary. But they're getting scared. They must have expected instant success or something. The longer this goes on the more afraid they are that the word will get out. And then their careers, their reputations, everything is on the line.''

"How much longer have I got?"

"You'll know by tomorrow morning,'' Ryder answered ominously.

"First, Lee, we're not getting proper intelligence. There has to be a base somewhere, a big one. Too big to have escaped notice. Second, we need those TOWs. You know what happened with the *Diogenes*. They know what happened—at least they know if they've seen the debriefing information I gave you. How do you expect us to eliminate boats full of pirates with a machine gun, some grenades and our automatic rifles?''

Barrabas turned away angrily, throwing his hand down. "Aw, hell. If that's all we can get, we can do it. My team can do it. But when there are TOWs lying around, and TOW mounts on the Huey, it'd be nice to have them, you know. Along with some interceptor decoys for the heat-sensitive missiles they threw at us last time around.''

"All that stuff is sitting in a warehouse out at the airbase,'' Ryder told him. "And if it were up to me, it would be on the chopper now. As for the intelligence, it's the best we've got.'' The rusty spring under the seat of the old office chair complained with a screech as the commander slowly sat back. He looked thoughtful.

"I already told you," he continued, "that the Red Vengeance is a secret society hundreds of years old. Its tentacles are said to spread deeply into all strata of society, including high-level people in the government, the military and even in the Royal Palace. It could be, Nile, that we're not getting all the information we should be getting."

Barrabas pushed himself up from the chair and grabbed his gloves from the table. As Ryder spoke, he had thought again of the two young Vietnamese girls he had met at the refugee camp. And he thought of that young woman, Drew, her father and the young man. Were they dead, he wondered. Or wishing for death in a place worse than hell?

"We'll get it," Barrabas said. "And we'll get them, TOWs or no TOWs." He flashed his gloves in an informal salute. "Thanks for the drink."

THE ISLAND WAS THE LARGEST of the Peril Islands, a large cluster of several hundred off the coast of Malaysia, almost five hundred kilometers southeast across the China Sea from Songkhla. So densely grouped were the islands, that from the air they looked like a solid landmass divided by rivers.

This particular island was shaped like a crescent at the end of a long gauntlet of small palm-covered islands and coral beachheads. A mountain, carpeted green with tropical forest, rose from the sandy shores. High, narrow waterfalls cut its sides, splashing a hundred meters down moss-covered surfaces of sheer rock.

Half a kilometer back from the shore, the mountain began its first steep incline before leveling slightly at a narrow plateau. An old stone fortress jutted from the contours of the rock, a two-hundred-year-old remnant of the rule of Chinese governors who once controlled traffic in the China Sea.

A high stone wall almost half a kilometer long paralleled the slope and joined the rocky hill at both ends. Inside the main gates was a long, narrow compound and beyond that the inner keep, a high stone building built straight back into the hillside. A village of several hundred palm-thatched houses on stilts ran along the beach. To one side lay a compound of metal warehouses surrounded by wire fences and guards. Long wharfs led from the shore to the deeper water, and small fishing boats were moored alongside them. Out in the bay the *Blood Maiden* floated serenely at anchor.

Ki Lim stood on the ramparts of the old fortress and looked out over his little kingdom. Technically the island was in an area disputed by three of the half dozen or so neighboring states, two decaying imperial powers in Europe and Red China.

Technicalities were easily removed, however, slipping away with the greasing of palms. All the right people in all the appropriate jurisdictions had been paid off. The issue was buried in the general morass of paperwork on the foreign ministry desks of the interested countries.

That left Ki Lim pretty much in charge of things, especially since the unfortunate death of his brother, the former Great Leader. The future of the Red Vengeance, as far as Ki Lim was concerned, was himself.

"These women with the blue eyes, Great Leader," Chung Hee said at an opportune moment. For his previous loyalty he was now a trusted adviser. It had been that way with Hum Lo, and with the Great Leader before that as well. Chung Hee had seen them come and go, each Great Leader having torn out the throat of the one before him. Only Chung Hee endured. "These women, there is still much talk from the captains that they will bring us ill luck. Of course, that is ridiculous." With the change in leadership, Chung Hee had quickly learned to scoff at superstition. "What is your interest in these women?" he asked Ki Lim, delicately stepping around the issue. The captains were edgy, and the ritual inauguration of the new leader had not yet taken place.

Ki Lim braced, sniffing the air of his little kingdom, surveying the village and the ship in the bay. They were standing at the long, narrow windows of the inner keep, which looked over the compound and past the outer walls.

"They fascinate me," he said. His voice was low, almost a hiss. "It's only a cultural difference. Because blue eyes don't exist in Asia, it's always been considered a sign of bad luck and ill fortune—the evil eye our grandfathers warned us about, which will turn us to stone. These women with blue eyes, they are my slaves. And yet, there is something about them that is...dangerous, some remnant of that childhood fear, I suppose."

He looked at Chung Hee, examining the pirate's face for a reaction. There was none. Chung Hee had long ago trained himself well to reveal no thoughts or opinions of his own. "That is exactly what the captains are muttering, Great Leader...."

"Bah. It's nonsense, of course. Just imagination. Fantasy. It lends an element of excitement to what I do with them in private."

Chung Hee bowed his head slightly in deference. He would not argue.

"But I have seen blue eyes that are clearly dangerous," Ki Lim said, turning to look out over the island again. "And they have been on my mind a great deal."

"Great Leader...?"

"This man I saw that night on the *Empress Christina*. He was young, and a warrior. Yet his hair was almost white, and his eyes were as blue as the great mountains of ice that sometimes drift south from the northern regions. He is dangerous. And danger intrigues me."

"But here, Ki Lim, he is not dangerous," Chung Hee assured him. "The Red Vengeance can find him and eliminate him at will."

"Perhaps." Ki Lim stroked his mustache and appeared deep in thought. "Perhaps, and yet he manages to show up just as we have overtaken the American yacht. I am sure it was him."

"It is only a matter of instructing our agents in the cities and the military to determine..."

"It's not necessary. I know. And I take a personal interest in his destruction."

"Then we will ascertain his whereabouts, take him, bring him to you...."

"But wouldn't it be more interesting if he were to come to me?" Ki Lim interrupted Chung Hee.

Chung Hee looked at the Great Leader wordlessly. Anything said would prove in the future to be foolhardy if he understood Ki Lim correctly.

The Great Leader began to pace, still stroking his thin, dark mustache. His obsidian pupils glinted with anticipation.

"It fascinates me to flirt this way," he said. He turned to Chung Hee, his mind made up. "Arrange it, brother! I want this man on his knees before me here. But I want him to come on his own. He and his helicopter will prove inadequate against our recently acquired missiles. As for the blue-eyed American woman, you will see that she is worth these murmurings of discontent. Tonight at the ritual ban-quiet, when I am confirmed as Great Leader, she shall be our entertainment.''

IT HAD BEEN A LONG, UNENDING NIGHTMARE—human cargo passing from boat to boat and long eternal nights in dark, stinking holds in the company of weeping girls and ship rats. Finally the women were bound inside huge cloth bags, thrown in the cargo net and unloaded over the side like a consignment of fish.

Drew Stevens felt herself being carried, then conveyed by truck over a bumpy, twisting road. After a brief journey over a hard, paved surface, they stopped. She was carried again and finally dumped from the cloth bag onto a straw-covered stone floor.

The room was a cell with high walls of enormous flattened stones. Near the ceiling on one side three narrow grates allowed a small amount of daylight to penetrate. There was nothing else except the straw. She looked around, examining her surroundings, and found herself staring into the astonished face of a blue-eyed Asian girl.

The girl slowly, cautiously, stretched out her hand and felt Drew's blond hair. She let it go as if it burned her.

''It's all right,'' Drew said. She picked up a handful of her hair and held it out.

Lac Sam eyed the American woman warily, but the strange blond hair proved irresistible. She touched it. It was real.

"Do you speak English?" Drew asked.

The girl held up her finger and thumb to show a little bit. Shyly she said, "You have blue eyes."

"Yes. I'm American. Where are you from?"

"You are American!" Lac Sam said excitedly. "I am from Vietnam. I have blue eyes, too. My father is American. Perhaps you know my father?"

Drew shook her head. Tears were suddenly streaming down Lac Sam's cheeks. Drew felt her own eyes scalding. She put her arms out, and the two women embraced each other for the small comfort there was to share between them.

That was Drew's introduction to the prisons of the Red Vengeance. Four days had passed since she had been brought there. She had kept careful track of the waning and fading of light at the grates near the stone ceiling and had estimated the time it took to bring her there at anywhere from three to five days. That meant it was a week or more that she'd been a prisoner.

In the dungeon she listened through the big iron door for outside sounds. Only occasionally was it opened. Twice a day to bring them food and to remove the bucket. Once a day when poor Lac Sam was summoned by her pirate master.

She had been unconscious when she'd been taken aboard the pirates' great ship, but other Vietnamese girls in the hold had told her that Kyle Carrington was still alive. Now she knew that the guards opened the iron door of a dungeon next to hers.

Once at night she awoke from a restless sleep and thought she heard him shouting. Suddenly his voice was cut off. She was never sure that she might not have imagined it. But she thought, hoped, that he was still alive.

Almost every day Lac Sam was taken from the cell and several hours later thrown back inside, bruised and exhausted. The young Vietnamese girl would sob, "I want to die. I want to die."

Drew would hug her and make her talk.

Lac Sam's master was a great pirate, a leader; she was certain of that. She was stripped and taken to his rooms where he made sport of her. He never touched her sexually, not like other women who were forced to be whores.

Her master terrorized her. Sometimes he put a bullet in a gun, spun the chambers, held it to her head and fired. The mock executions gave him great pleasure. Once he made her stand for hours without moving in a cage containing a deadly poisonous snake. On another occasion he set fire to her long hair, only to throw ice-cold water on her before the flames spread to her scalp and face.

When she was terrorized into abject exhaustion to the point of collapse or hysterical screaming, she was taken away.

"I want to die," she would moan to Drew. And sometimes Drew felt the same way, although her ordeal had yet to begin.

It was afternoon, she reckoned, on the seventh, eighth or ninth day. Lac Sam had been taken several hours earlier. Drew waited, knowing she would have to comfort the poor girl when she was returned to the cell. She heard the distant thudding of heavy doors being closed, which signaled Lac Sam's return. She stood quickly and pressed herself against the wall beside the door. When it was opened, she would have a few brief moments to see beyond the cell. Each time she prayed to catch a glimpse of Kyle. The stone corridor was poorly lit. Usually she only saw guards shuffling about and laughing at stupid jokes.

She listened carefully. The door to the adjacent dungeon was being opened. A moment later she heard movement outside her own door and hands on the lock.

She moved forward just a few inches, her eyes straining against the gloom. Her stomach fluttered. The other prisoner in the other cell was being taken out.

Two guards, holding Lac Sam between them, blocked the view completely. They threw the young Vietnamese girl roughly into the dungeon. Just as they backed off and swung the door shut, Drew saw the prisoner. One of the tall blond man's arms ended in a clean white bandage.

Kyle.

He was still alive.

He turned and saw her face through the narrow crack just as the door was slammed shut. His legs were chained, and two pirates held him on each side. He shouted and tried to jump away from them. Quickly they subdued him and carried him off.

Drew heard his shouts and the fading sounds of struggle through the closed door of her cell. The knowledge that he was living rang like a note of hope.

She turned to Lac Sam who lay on the floor where she had been thrown. She sobbing uncontrollably. Drew put her arms around her and hugged her closely.

"There now," she said soothingly. "It's all right. You're with me now."

Lac Sam's tiny body shuddered, and her sobs grew louder. She struggled from Drew's arms and looked at her fearfully, her cheeks strewn with the wet lines of her many tears.

"No, Drew. Not all right. Not all right at all." Lac Sam shook her head in utter negation.

"What's the matter, Lac Sam? Whatever are you saying?" Drew came closer, trying again to comfort the almost hysterical girl.

"No, Drew. This time master say that he will call for you to come. Tonight."

Drew shivered. She felt the clammy, bony hand of an imagined future grip behind her neck, and the memory of what had brought her to this fortress of doom tightened like an iron knot in her stomach.

12

Barrabas woke suddenly, cued by an inner biological alarm that never failed him. His eyes opened, confronting the brown water stains and curling paint on the ceiling. He was lying on his back on the hard, narrow bed in the Golden Paradise Hotel. A couple of seconds later the tiny backup alarm in his chronometer began its persistent beep. He turned it off, sat up and planted his feet firmly on the floor.

The thick yellow light of late afternoon sliced through the louvered shutters running along the window. Blades of sun striped the floor, the dingy rug, the bed and the faded wallpaper. The hot, unending steam bath of the tropics had resumed, and everything was already damp.

After his meeting with Ryder, Barrabas had returned to the little hotel and fallen into a deep dreamless sleep. Four hours of it. Enough to rest the muscles and the mind sufficiently to start again. The mercs were set to start another evening reconnaissance at 1800 hours. He'd been running that kind of schedule—grabbing four hours of sleep between operations lasting anywhere from eight to twenty hours—for a week now.

When it was all over, the crash would come. He'd sleep for a solid week. But that was the future: when Songkhla and the Red Vengeance were over and done with. He had slept in his khaki trousers and an undershirt. The shirt was damp from the humidity and his sweat. He peeled it off and splashed cold water on his face and arms at the little sink, then he grabbed a clean T-shirt from his duffel bag and one of the neatly pressed shirts that hung by the door. The proprietor's faithful wife always made sure he had a clean supply. The short-sleeved khaki shirts were military style with epaulets and button-down pockets, but lacked identifying badges and insignia.

Nile Barrabas and the SOB. Covert action, unofficial style. The no-name boys.

He lifted the heavy holster with his Canadian-made Browning Hi-Power and strapped it around his waist. Now it was real.

He had just reached for his black steel-toed boots when there was a little knock on the door.

"Come in!" Barrabas tucked his pant leg into the top of a boot and tightened the laces. The door opened, and the little proprietor greeted him with the usual big smile and slight, nodding bow of the head.

"You sleep good, Mr. Barra-Bas?" He pronounced the colonel's name with the stress on the last syllable.

"Fine, U-Thee."

The proprietor moved aside and his wife came forward from behind him, bearing a little tray and a steaming cup of coffee. She set the cup down on the table and quickly tiptoed out. The proprietor smiled and bowed again. "I come tell you when car arrive."

Barrabas liked the shabby old hotel near the Songkhla port. The majority of the guests seemed to be young heavily made-up Asian ladies who entertained a variety of foreign boyfriends. They stayed clear of Barrabas, perhaps because the owner warned them away.

The Thai couple were friendly, sincere, honest— and they knew everything that went on in their little establishment. It was like having a security system thrown in for the price of the room. His shirts came back every day, freshly laundered and pressed, and a cup of strong hot coffee was waiting for him whenever he was ready to start again.

He took advantage of the few extra minutes to drink the coffee and do some exercises, stretching the tendons of his legs, arms, torso and neck. The long hours in the chopper tightened everything. He webbed his fingers and pushed them outward to crack the knuckles. He flexed them. Then he flexed his trigger finger by itself. It was an important member of the team. His favorite.

Five minutes later there was another little knock on the door. He threw back the last of the coffee as the proprietor pushed his way in again.

"Car is here," U-Thee nodded graciously.

Barrabas nodded and grabbed the lined leather jacket from the chair and made his way out of the hotel. Outside, Nate Beck was waiting at the wheel of a jeep.

"Personally I prefer the penthouse at the Hilton," Beck said as Barrabas climbed in. "There's nothing like a hot tub or a sauna after one of our runs. Everyone else will be waiting at the hangar for us."

Nate Beck drove slowly through the narrow streets of the port quarter, heading for the southern outskirts of Songkhla. The city was caught momentarily in the lull between afternoon and evening when the population disappeared indoors to eat and to refresh after the day's torpor. The cooler evenings offered a slight respite from the heat.

The late light from the low sun played slowly, tenderly, along the stone surfaces of the great fortress that crowned the city. The towers and walls fell into a high relief of sunlight and dark shadow. Once impregnable, the fortress now squatted on its hillside like n ancient circus elephant in honorable retirement.

The technology of war had long superseded it. The stone walls that had once defied invaders and had symbolized the might of the ruling governors now looked like a laughable folly from times past. Two centuries of progress had turned it from stronghold to deathtrap. One well-directed nonnuclear missile would reduce it from fortress to ruin.

"Any word on the TOWs?" Beck asked as he turned the jeep onto the road that led through the hills on the southern flank of the old fortress. They were heading for the plateau that leveled out above the hills behind the city.

"Ryder says he's still working on them." Barrabas stopped short of mentioning the problems the commander was having with the Thai navy brass. The mercs didn't need that kind of discouragement.

Several minutes later the airfield and hangars came into view. Something was wrong. Two identical jeeps were parked outside the gates. The SOBs stood around, talking with the armed Thai guards. The mercs looked angry. The Thais stood stiff and impassive, a half dozen of them, blocking entrance to the airfield.

Nate pulled in between the other two jeeps, and Claude Hayes strolled over to the passenger side to speak to the colonel.

"They're not letting us in," the big black American said in his slow, laconic drawl. "They say they got orders."

Hayes never seemed ruffled. Nanos, on the other hand, was shouting. Then he gave the impassive guards an impressive view of his raised index finger. When he saw Barrabas, he raced over.

"They got orders. We got work to do. Let's just slam in there. Those gates can't hold three jeeps back. If they get in the way, it's their tough luck."

"Hold on, Alex," Barrabas said quietly. "Let's get on the blower to Ryder and find out what's going on first."

He reached for the modular telephone in the storage compartment between the front seats just as it started to beep. He picked it up and clicked it on. It was Ryder. "I was just about to call you," Barrabas said solemnly.

Ryder was excited. "Nile, you won't believe what came across my desk this afternoon."

"An order to close down the mission."

"What? No, not at all. The brass is still balking, but they haven't decided anything yet."

"Tell that to the guards who won't let us inside the gates of the airfield right now."

"No? Shit. You're serious?"

"Dead serious."

There was a momentary silence on the line.

"Wait right there. I'll be out as fast as I can."

Barrabas restrained his own anger. "We're not going anywhere, Lee." He clicked off the phone and put it back in the compartment.

Twenty minutes later Ryder's military car tore up the road on the side of the plateau just as the sun hit the western horizon like a big neon gumdrop. The driver braked behind the row of jeeps outside the gates. Barrabas walked over just as Ryder opened the door.

"Get in," he told Barrabas. "And close the door."

"Did you find out what the hell's going on?" Barrabas demanded, slipping in beside Ryder in the rear seat.

"Yup. One little tight-assed admiral got nervous and jumped the gun. Now the others are going along with it. Let's deal with that in a minute. Look at this."

He handed Barrabas a red folder with Classified A1 clearly marked in Thai and English. Inside was a single-page intelligence report. Barrabas scanned it quickly. It was a summary of certain satellite information supplied by a top-secret American agency.

The agency's reconnaissance and intelligence divisions suspected major smuggling activity in the Peril Islands. The satellite photographs had picked up what appeared to be a supply base. A small fishing town had an unusual number of warehouses and deep-water port facilities much more sophisticated than anything normally required in such a thinly populated, isolated region. And subsequent reconnaissance had shown the arrivals and departures of a number of large boats.

The Thai and Malaysian governments had been notified through normal diplomatic channels. The recommendation of the Thai foreign ministry was that the information be disregarded. No reason was given.

"Where did this come from?" Barrabas asked. He shifted the intelligence report aside. The next page was a photocopied map of the region marking the Peril Islands and designating the area of activity.

Ryder shook his head. "It was on my desk when I came in late this afternoon. Want to draw your own conclusions, or shall I tell you mine?"

"Tell me yours first."

"The Red Vengeance is reputed to have agents in very high places. That's how this information was buried at the Foreign Ministry. But the group of military officers who secretly approved your team's covert action against the pirates also have well-placed allies. One of them must have come across this and leaked it to us."

It was Barrabas's turn to shake his head. "It doesn't make sense, Lee. If these came to us legitimately—I mean by someone on our side—then what are these guards doing telling us we can't go in there."

"Tell me your idea."

"I dunno." Barrabas looked at the papers in his hand. "I think you're right about the first part. The Red Vengeance has agents everywhere. They also know we're after them. They want us to come for them, so they're feeding us the information."

"A setup?"

"Or a dare." He jerked his head toward the gate. The mercs were still standing around, silent but with growing anger. "There'd be no harm in us checking it out. But what about this mess? Any ideas."

"I can work on the brass. This new information gives me some leverage. But it'll take..."

"A day? Two days? A week? Sorry, Lee. I can't hold my soldiers that long. If we're going to do it, it's now or never."

Ryder sat back, silent and thoughtful for a moment as Barrabas waited for him to respond to the ultimatum.

"You and your people have left some personal equipment in the hangar, haven't you?

"Not really. All the hardware, but it's Thai navy issue."

"Let's say you did. I can get you through the gates to pick it up. Once we're inside, well...there aren't many guards at this base. What you see here, and maybe a few more inside. And some mechanics and workmen."

Barrabas saw immediately what Ryder was getting at. He rolled down the window and beckoned Claude Hayes to come over. When the black man was close to the window, the colonel said quietly, "We're going in there to pick up our personal belongings through Commander Ryder's good graces, but we're not leaving without the helicopter. Tell the others to be ready. Move when they see me move."

Hayes nodded once and moved away.

Barrabas rolled up the window.

"Nile." Ryder looked at him, tapping his chin with his finger. "You're going to have to make it look real."

Barrabas laughed. "Not too real. You'll never get up again."

It took Commander Ryder several minutes to arrange for the gates to be opened. The guards insisted on contacting their superiors in Songkhla.

Barrabas sauntered over to where the mercs were standing. "Alex, Lee and Billy Two, I want you to stay here by the gate. When you hear a single shot, disable the guards and boot it over to the ordnance warehouse. If someone's not there to meet you, open it up."

Finally permission was granted. The procession of jeeps and Ryder's car passed through.

The Huey was parked under the corrugated tin roof of a large hangar with open sides at the far end of the field. Men in mechanics' overalls were working on it. Two of them were carefully stenciling Thai navy markings back on the sides. Another had just replaced the TOW missiles in the carriers on either side of the fuselage.

"This could be our lucky day after all," Barrabas murmured to Nate as the jeep stopped.

He and Nate got out. Claude Hayes and Jeff Bishop left the other jeep as Ryder's car pulled in behind. The mercs moved nonchalantly toward the helicopter.

Barrabas waited for Commander Ryder to get out of his car. Their eyes met briefly as Ryder stood up and closed the door. Barrabas balled his fist and slammed it into the commander's face.

The American naval attaché went out like a light bulb, slumping backward against the car and sliding to the ground. With his other arm, Barrabas reached into the driver's open window and grabbed the chauffeur by his collar. He jerked the young Thai soldier's head and shoulders out and slammed a fist into his temple. The driver's head bounced, and he hung limp and unconscious over the car door.

Barrabas pulled out his 9 mm pistol and fired a shot into the air.

At the helicopter, Hayes, Bishop and Nanos had made short work of the mechanic and the two painters. Each chose a target and dropped him before he knew what was happening. They grabbed their unconscious victims by the feet and dragged them away from the chopper.

"Geoff, get it warmed up. Claude, check the fuel and those mountings on the TOWs." The colonel pointed across the airfield to the large warehouse. "You can pick us up by the ordnance warehouse."

The other jeep was heading up from the gate. "Nate, let's go!"

Beck floored the four-wheel and tore across the landing strip, meeting Nanos, Hatton and Billy Two at the metal garage doors in the side of the building. The doors had thick, heavy padlocks strung through steel clasps.

"Anybody got a key?" Alex shouted. The Greek was antsy on the adrenaline hit.

"Didn't have time," Lee replied, swinging her Walther P-38 out of her holster. With cool, smooth precision, she worked her way down the first door, firing away the locks.

Billy Two and Nanos rushed forward and swung the door open.

The warehouse was dark, and the fading evening light provided no illumination. Lee Hatton moved inside and found light switches. The mercs were confronted by an enormous field of crated weapons and ammo cases.

"I want BARB interceptors and portable launchers," Barrabas told them, moving into the warehouse. "Ryder told me they were here, so fan out and look until we find them."

From the other side of the airfield came the steady whopping sound of the chopper's rotors. Its running lights came on, then it rose several feet into the air and hovered a few seconds before moving forward from the hangar; then it veered up and flew across the airfield.

Most of the hardware in the warehouse was American; the contents of the crates were carefully labeled in U.S. military code. The mercs were familiar with it from their experience in the services. In less than a minute they heard Lee Hatton shout.

Billy Two appeared at her side with a crowbar and quickly opened the top of the crate. The two-foot-long BARB interceptors lay packed together, four to a row. Hayes and Nanos moved as a team nearby. Hayes used a crowbar to pry the tops off while Nanos searched the contents.

Finally they found the portable launchers. The shiny tubes were only a little longer than the missiles they were meant to launch, with a trigger mechanism a third of the way down one end.

Suddenly the long wail of an alarm sounded from the gate. Other sirens from different corners of the airfield joined in unison. Someone had regained consciousness.

"Get them out of here!" Barrabas yelled. The mercs hoisted the heavy crates, two men on each one, and dog-walked them to the door of the warehouse just as Bishop brought the Huey to hover outside.

Some military vehicles had come up the road to the isolated airfield and stopped at the gates. Barrabas could hear the noise and commotion as the new arrivals discovered the unconscious guards. Their engines revved up again, and the headlights moved quickly across the airfield toward the mercs.

Bullets were next if they didn't get their asses out of there.

"Get aboard, on the double!" Barrabas shouted. He flicked off the lights of the warehouse at the same time that Bishop turned off the chopper's lights. The mercs hoisted the crates into the fuselage and dived in.

Bishop raised the collective, and the helicopter lifted into a hover as Barrabas raced from the door of the warehouse. Across the landing strip orange muzzle flashes were visible in the darkness. He felt bullets wing past, lacing the air around his head like steel wires. He jumped for the rear door of the Huey. The arms of his soldiers reached down to grab and pull him up.

The helicopter rose quickly until it cleared the top of the warehouse. It angled, veering back and away from the Thai navy attackers as it gained altitude. Barrabas felt something hard and heavy slam into his boot, twisting his ankle as he pulled himself in the last few feet.

"Awright!" a jubilant Nanos shouted. "We left them chomping our tracks!"

Below them the lights of the isolated airport grew distant in the darkness at the edge of the bright coastal city. Bishop turned the Huey out to sea.

Barrabas looked at his boot. A bullet had gone through the thick sole, leaving a perfect circular indentation in the rubber.

"Hot foot!" Claude Hayes muttered over the colonel's shoulder. "You weren't running fast enough."

"Just fast enough," Barrabas corrected. "Remind me not to slow down."

Hayes laughed. "Next on the agenda is a midnight rendezvous with the Red Vengeance. Is that correct?" he asked.

"That's right, Claude," Barrabas said, standing and putting his weight on the foot that had almost bought it. The impact of the bullet had snapped the foot sideways, slightly bruising the ankle.

"Sounds to me like they're expecting us, too," Lee said.

"Yeah, but look what we got in store for them," Nanos crowed. "Eight TOW missiles, four to a side."

"Hmph," Billy Two grunted cynically. "What I want to know is what they have in store for us."

Barrabas went forward to the cockpit and took the copilot's seat beside Bishop.

"How long will it take us to get there?" Barrabas asked.

"Three hours, give or take ten or twenty minutes."

"You can find this place at night?"

"I studied that little map and some of the charts I have here pretty carefully. There are pretty distinctive landmarks, including the shape and location of some of the islands, that'll mark the way. When we get close enough, the lights of that little town will act as a beacon."

The chopper was over the Gulf of Thailand and heading south to the China Sea. The lights of Songkhla grew smaller until they were nothing more than a thin golden necklace strung in darkness along the distant shore behind them. Barrabas rode a long way without saying anything until Bishop spoke up.

"What's on your mind, Colonel?"

"What Billy Two said a while ago."

"What's that?"

"The Red Vengeance. Wondering what they have in store for us."

WHEN KYLE CARRINGTON RETURNED to consciousness, he found that it was impossible to move.

His head was tightly attached to something by leather straps across the chin, around his neck and around his head at eyebrow level. The rest of his body was squashed together, his knees pushed up against his chest and his bent arms pressed tightly against his sides.

He was naked, in a little box. His head projected just slightly above it and was covered by a thick, dark cloth that cut out all light. It tickled his nose and made him want to sneeze. His arm, where the hand had been severed, was numb from the painkiller his jailors had injected into it.

He was aware of people outside, gruff, faraway voices, and then he felt a hand roughly ruffle his hair. He heard the sound of a little machine being turned on. The little machine buzzed in close to his ear like an electric mosquito. He felt the warm metal vibrate against his scalp, swooping up along the contours of his skull, shearing his hair off.

He tried to struggle, but movement was impossible. Thick leather straps tightened around his body. And the band that reached from his eyebrows to the back of his cranium was metal, not leather. Two metal knobs pushed threateningly against the back of his cheekbones near his ears. His head was as rigidly fixed as a pole buried in the ground.

He wanted to scream, to scare them off maybe, anything to make them stop what they were doing to him. It rose from his throat and slammed into a hard leather knob in his mouth that forced his teeth apart.

He felt needles being carefully injected into his scalp and then a quickly growing numbness. Kyle Carrington stopped. He sat there, frightened, quiet and still, and paid total, committed attention to whatever it was that was going on around him.

And he prayed. Oh, Jesus, did he pray.

13

For four hours the SOBs flew across the Gulf of Thailand and over the China Sea. They rode silently, each fighter focused inward by the deeply hypnotic vibrations of the Huey. They rode without lights, entrusting their lives in the dark belly of the old chopper to Geoff Bishop's navigational instincts.

The pilot's hands rested lightly on the cyclic control and the collective. From time to time he made delicate adjustments, treading the antitorque pedals lightly, moving the collective up or down to change altitude, fine-tuning the throttle, shifting direction by a slight turn of the cyclic control.

Every ten minutes he stretched, almost imperceptibly tensing his muscles, making them work against one another in the seat, then relaxing. The mesmerizing effect of helicopter vibrations could be deadeningly dangerous to the pilot. From time to time he opened the little vent window, letting the hard, cold air pound into his face, invigorating him like a slap of ice water.

Barrabas sat next to him, still, never turning, his steel-blue eyes staring ahead.

The sky was moonless, wispy white with stars that gradually rotated across the horizon during the hours it took the mercs to approach their destination. A thin band of reflected light separated ocean from sky. Sometimes, below, the tiny jeweled lights of an ocean liner twinkled as it sailed by.

It was almost 2300 hours when they spotted the Peril Islands, a series of low, dark bumps on the edge of the horizon. Soon they were over the first of them.

The dark landmasses floated on the gray ocean and stretched away to each side. There were hundreds of islands, some only a few rocks and a palm tree. Others were larger jungle-covered islands fringed with beaches. Little yellow lights indicated the presence of fishing villages.

The clusters of islands were separated by a natural channel that ran through them like a long, wide canal. The avenue of water swept ahead through the Peril Islands for miles. And far ahead was the biggest island of them all. The great dark bulk of a mountain rose black against the night, silhouetted by a thin silver band of light from the starry sky. Halfway down, lights sparkled at the windows of a fortress, in the town spread along the beach and in the portholes of the *Blood Maiden*, anchored serenely among the fishing boats in the little harbor.

TWO MEN CAME FOR DREW just as the evening light outside the tiny barred window began to fade. With her hands tied tightly behind her back, she was hurried along damp stone corridors and up long flights of concrete steps. She hoped against all odds that she might see Kyle again, if only briefly, but the broad corridors and passages were deserted. Although she tried hard to memorize the labyrinthine route, it was impossible.

At best she knew she was being kept in some great stone building. Her guards were taking her higher. The air was fresher, and the occasional slit in the stone walls admitted the smell of the sea.

The guards came to an abrupt halt at a stout wooden door halfway down a long, wide corridor that ran the length of the fortress. A third pirate, a swarthy, overweight man, was waiting for them.

Barely stopping to look at her, the big man grabbed Drew by the back of her neck and squeezed, forcing her to her knees. She felt his rough hands under her chin yanking her hair back. Then a leather band was pulled around her throat and tightened. His big hand slapped into the small of her back. pushing her forward onto her hands and knees.

One of the other guards knocked on the door.

The big swarthy man attached something to the back of the collar. It was a chain. He yanked it, pulling Drew's head back, and grunted.

Slowly the door swung open.

The room was elaborately appointed with rich oriental carpets on the floor and ornate tapestries covering the stone walls. At the far end enormous cushions were piled around a great divan. A long, low table held a tall brass samovar. Nearby, a short, thin Asian watched Drew curiously, unconsciously stroking his long, thin mustache. His glinting obsidian eyes were as dark as death.

The burly guard who held the leash grunted again and shoved Drew forward with his foot. She tried to get up, but his foot came forward again and kicked her down. Once again Drew tried to rise. The pirate yelled gruffly and yanked the leash. Drew spilled over backward and collapsed. She lay on her side on the floor, her body shuddering. She sobbed, miserable in her helplessness.

Ki Lim watched impassively from twenty meters away. He ordered the guard to let the woman come on her own. Then, in almost perfect English, he addressed her.

"You can walk, woman."

Drew looked up, surprised to suddenly hear English spoken. She wiped her eyes and slowly rose to her feet. The leash hung down her back and trailed several feet on the floor.

"Come," Ki Lim urged her. "Yes, I speak English. Fluently. I studied at a British university once, before I returned to my people and took up...the age-old profession of piracy."

She stepped cautiously, suspecting a trick.

"Come along, woman. I won't hurt you . . . yet."

She went forward until she stood about six feet from the little Asian. The guards followed behind.

Ki Lim smiled and circled her slowly, looking her up and down. Her pants and blouse were torn and soiled from her capture and imprisonment. He poked at her, pulling back her collar and the ripped edges of fabric to feel her skin. Then he came in front of her and grasped her chin in a viselike grip.

Drew tensed, sucking her breath in sharply, not sure of what to suspect, but fearing the unspeakable.

He held her head close to his and stared, full of hatred and fascination, into her deep blue eyes.

"Pretty, pretty," he mumbled. He thrust her head sharply away. His lips curled in contempt.

"Your blue eyes excite me."

Drew shivered. The creepy little man emanated a strange, dark energy.

"Wh-who are you?" she asked fearfully.

Ki Lim's eyes lit up, and he laughed. "I am the leader of the Red Vengeance, the pirates who seized your boat. And you, my dear, are my slave. Tell me your name. Are you American?"

Drew was silent.

"Yes?" he said impatiently.

"D-D-Drew," she said. "Y-yes, I'm American. Let me go, please!" Her tragic wail curled pleadingly through the huge room.

Ki Lim threw his head back and laughed.

Abruptly he became serious, his brow furrowing, and he eyed her darkly. "You will never be let go. Whoever, whatever you were before you became my prisoner, is over forever. Gone. As if it never existed."

Ki Lim walked close to her again. She lowered her head, unable to look at her captor. He stuck his face close and looked into her eyes again. "Your life from now on is nothing other than what I decide it will be."

Drew shivered, tight with fear.

"Wh-what will you do with me?" she asked in a small voice.

"Entertain myself," Ki Lim replied without hesitation. "And when you no longer amuse me I will allow you to die. You are privileged, really. I could have simply given you to my crew."

He circled around her, leering.

"Twenty or thirty men at a time. You'd like that wouldn't you?" he said, sticking his face close to hers once again and watching her eyes intently.

"As it is," Ki Lim continued, "you are about to be honored. A rare honor. In just a few moments, at a great banquet, I will be confirmed as the Great Leader of the Red Vengeance in a secret ritual. It's a simple idea really. There are certain things we do together that are so...unusual.... The participants are forever chained together in a sacred bond. No one outside of our secret organization has witnessed the ritual in hundreds of years—and lived to tell."

He stopped circling and stood with his hands behind his back, rocking slightly with a satisfied air. "Nor will you, although you will live longer than some."

"Kyle," Drew said, suddenly, desperately brave. "What have you done to Kyle?"

Ki Lim looked at her for a moment somewhat puzzled. "Kyle? Ah, yes, is that his name? Kyle? Oh, he'll be there, too. Don't worry, my dear. You'll see him. He's being prepared for the grand occasion right now."

"COLONEL?" Bishop asked, breaking the silence in the helicopter.

"I know. I see it," Barrabas said, staring ahead at the island looming bigger and bigger on the approaching horizon.

Bishop reached out and flicked a toggle. In the fuselage a small red light went on. The mercs looked up. It was time.

Nate Beck swung open the side door, letting a blast of the cold air sock into the cabin.

Nanos shivered as he grabbed one of the BARB disposable launchers. "Hope this baby does the trick."

Nate and Hayes fed the M-60 while Billy Two and Lee Hatton loaded the BARBs, carefully placing the launchers near the side door. Nanos distributed mags of 5.56 mm bullets to the mercs.

In the cockpit Barrabas put the earphones over his head and adjusted the tiny transmitter a few inches from his mouth. He raised his infrared light-intensification binoculars and scanned the fortress and the hillside behind it. There were several areas in the darkness that he noted as potential trouble spots.

There was no doubt in his mind that the Red Vengeance was waiting for them. The invitation would not have been issued if the pirates weren't certain of adequate defenses to knock out a single covert action team in a helicopter.

Heat-directed missiles were the best the pirates could get. Barrabas had seen them use one, and only the explosion aboard the *Diogenes* had saved the mercs.

"We're inside their radar range now," Bishop said, glancing up from the control panel. Even as he finished talking, a small light began flashing. "Yup. We've just detected it. We're on their screen now."

Barrabas gave his final order to the pilot.

"Get in there as fast and with as high an altitude as you can. And let them shoot first."

WHEN HE WAS FINISHED HIS AUDIENCE, Ki Lim ordered Drew taken away. Once again the young American woman found herself being pushed through the long, dark corridors of the strange building. When they stopped, she was shoved into a large white-tiled room that was very hot and humid.

There were other women present, Asian women who spoke no English.

Her clothes were stripped from her, and she was plunged into a hot bath. After that she was dried, then dressed in a long diaphanous blue robe that did nothing to conceal her nakedness.

Only the collar around her neck stayed put. Her hair was combed back and tied at her neck. A young Vietnamese girl came forward and shyly offered her a handful of makeup—some lipstick and kohl. Drew was afraid to put it on, afraid to make herself look beautiful, and yet she was just as frightened of the pirates' wrath if she failed to please them.

The women brought her a mirror. She sat on the little chair and applied the makeup lightly to her face. The women withdrew to wait for what seemed like a very long time.

Eventually the guards came back, as coarse and brutal as ever. Once again the chain was hooked through the collar. Laughing and guffawing, they pulled her from the room.

This time the guards seemed in a hurry. They led her through the dimly lit fortress until they came to two enormous carved wooden doors, twice as high as a man. Pirates standing outside took hold of the big brass handles. The doors swung smoothly outward.

The sounds of feasting and merrymaking burst forth.

Drew was pushed through.

She stumbled forward into a great hall. The high-vaulted ceiling was hung with great red banners bearing Chinese letters in gold cloth. Dozens of richly dressed men sat along the low dining tables that ran up both sides and along the end. The tables were heaped with food and large glass pitchers of rice wine. The pirates were shouting, cheering and applauding.

Ki Lim stood at the head table at the end of the room, smiling at his colleagues on both sides. He wore a Chinese coat of black brocade. Suspended on a chain from his neck was a silver oval with a blue center. It looked like an eye.

He was in the midst of a speech.

Drew felt a rough, powerful hand on the back of her neck again. The guard squeezed and picked her up. She skimmed the floor as the guard walked her forward and placed her ten feet in front of Ki Lim.

There was an iron bolt set into the stone floor. The guard jerked the chain on Drew's collar, forcing her down. He ran the chain through the bolt in the floor and locked it in place.

"This is the woman who has caused you to whisper rumors of fear and danger among yourselves," Ki Lim addressed the captains of the Red Vengeance. "Look at her. Does she look dangerous? Does she look like she can cause the least bit of harm to any of you?"

Their cheering ended, and there was a low murmur throughout the great hall. The pirate captains consulted one another in whispers.

Chung Hee entered the hall from a door somewhere behind the head table. The older, white-haired Chinese went directly to Ki Lim and whispered urgently in his ear, "There is an alert."

Ki Lim kept his eyes on his audience as if he had not heard. He raised his arm and waved toward Drew. "Look at the blue-eyed woman. Watch her. See for yourselves that she is totally at my mercy. Discuss this with your brothers, and if you still fear her—" Ki Lim paused for effect and lifted his goblet of rice wine into the air "—then perhaps you too had best wear skirts and be quartered with the women!"

He toasted his own challenge and gulped back a mouthful of wine. The captains' deafening laughter filled the hall. Goblets were lifted and wine was downed.

Ki Lim stepped back and moved nearer to Chung Hee.

"What is it?"

"Our radar has picked up an object coming toward us at great speed. It appears to be a helicopter."

"So soon? Curious," Ki Lim said. "Well, we are prepared."

"The Great Leader knows best," Chung Hee said nervously.

"It is impossible for a single helicopter to escape heat-sensitive missiles. Let them come for me in my lair and they will be destroyed! The explosion of a helicopter in midair will provide spectacular fireworks to celebrate my investiture as Great Leader. It is the gift of gratitude I have planned to give to my captains on this occasion."

"And a wonderful gift," Chung Hee assured Ki Lim doubtfully.

"Is everything ready? Is the young American prepared?"

"Yes, Great Leader. We await only your word."

"Excellent. In a moment the missiles shall destroy this man with blue eyes who troubles my existence." Ki Lim turned back to face the assembled pirates of the Red Vengeance. "My brothers!" he cried, raising his goblet again, "Let the ritual begin!"

KYLE CARRINGTON'S BODY ACHED from his cramped position in the small box. After the sharp little pricks in his scalp, he realised he was being injected with a hypodermic syringe. Each time it pierced the skin, he was aware of the quickly growing numbness from a local anesthetic.

Soon all sensation above his eyebrows was gone. He was shivering uncontrollably and covered with sweat.

Now the busy hands outside the dark box had taken a sharp, pointed object and were drawing a line around his head, level with the metal band that held him in place. He felt a liquid warmth seep through to his cheeks, run down his nose and tickle the back of his neck.

Then the buzzing electric instrument approached, and his skull began to vibrate, driving conscious thought from his brain. A spine-shattering electronic noise rippled through his body.

The hands outside were moving something in a slow circle around his cranium. The acrid odor of burning calcium filled his tiny prison, a smell familiar from the dentist's chair, when bone was being drilled at high speed. He began to tremble rapidly, and little inarticulate noises escaped from his throat.

When the electric machine had completed its encircling of his head, it stopped as suddenly as it had begun. The skin along the metal band stung painfully despite the anesthetic.

He was conscious and thinking lucidly. He couldn't imagine what they were doing to him.

He told himself to relax, that it would all be over soon enough. But he heard the involuntary whimpers of a highly frightened animal clawing at his throat. He tried to move, to struggle again, but it was impossible. He was held fast in the tiny box by the leather straps and the iron band around his head.

The hands that had probed his head stopped. They had gone. He listened, but heard nothing. Then, far away, he heard a door open and a burst of noise.

Someone was making a speech. He couldn't understand the language. There was a burst of laughter and loud applause. Rapid footsteps approached.

Suddenly Kyle Carrington saw daylight. Someone ripped the thick, dark cloth away from his face. For a moment he saw that, yes, he was imprisoned up to his neck in a small wooden box. Steel rods screwed into mountings supported the steel band and knobs that held his head firmly in place.

A little Asian man wearing a blood-spattered white coat bent down and looked directly into Carrington's eyes. He laughed, dully and unfastened the leather strap that held the gag in the American's mouth. When the gag was pulled away, Kyle Carrington tried to scream.

A tiny croak emerged from his throat. He tried again. Another croak. He felt the waves of panic building in his chest, and his body involuntarily straining against the bonds that held him.

The man moved behind Carrington and placed a cover of some kind over his entire head, plunging him once again into darkness.

The little box shook. Someone had grabbed one end.

It moved. It was on wheels.

The laughter and applause grew louder as Kyle Carrington felt himself rolling closer and closer to its source.

14

Geoff Bishop piloted the chopper to the right of the Red Vengeance fortress.

"Distance?" Barrabas demanded.

"Just under a kilometer and getting closer."

The colonel lifted the image-intensification binoculars and scanned the dark hillside behind the fortress.

"Veer left," he told Bishop. "Parallel the face of the fortress and the hill."

He shifted in his seat. Through the glasses a white spark suddenly appeared on the hill and quickly faded. There was a second flash nearby.

"Enemy fire, one o'clock and eleven o'clock," he said calmly, directing his words to the transmitter by his mouth. He pushed it away and spoke to the pilot. "Geoff, hold your course steady."

In the fuselage Alex, Lee and Billy Two straddled the floor of the Huey on their stomachs. Each of them sighted down the long steel tube of a BARB portable launcher. As soon as Barrabas spoke from the cockpit, they pulled the triggers.

The brief, hollow discharge pounded like a baton on a kettle drum, and the recoil knocked each of them back a foot and a half from the edge.

The small, yard-long missiles shot out. The initial firing caused a tiny pair of thin wires to snap from the neck of each missile. Inside the steel body, electronic chips activated, seeking out nearby heat sources and directing the missile. At the same time a heat-intensification device turned on, heating the steel body to a super-hot temperature and attracting heat-sensitive projectiles.

Almost instantaneously two midair explosions a quarter of a kilometer off the side of the helicopter lit up the night. Bishop's right hand gripped the cyclic control, and he fought to adjust the pitch angle of the main rotor as concussion waves rolled over the chopper.

"Yeeehawww!" The Greek whooped once for the home run.

"Twelve o'clock," Barrabas spoke urgently into the transmitter again.

The mercs in the fuselage had thrown aside their empty launchers and grabbed new ones. Alex and Lee fired, and again a brief orange explosion flickered and died.

"Ten o'clock!" Barrabas said quickly.

Billy Two fired. His shot was followed quickly by another from Lee.

The explosion was immediate and almost directly below them. The helicopter heaved upward on the brutal waves and slammed down like an elevator with a broken cable.

"Head in real close now," Barrabas told Bishop.

The Canadian fought with the Huey's controls, yanking the collective up and turning the throttle to raise the rpm. He shifted the cyclic, and the chopper angled suddenly to the right. He lowered the cockpit and raised the tail for the correct angle of attack, then he zeroed in on the hillside half a kilometer ahead.

Barrabas pushed the transmitter and earphones off his head and reached for the FLIR sites overhead. Now that the pirates had had the opportunity to shoot first, their land-based launchers would be hot.

The FLIR equipment, Forward Looking Infrared, picked up the highly distinctive heat emissions. All Barrabas had to do was decide on his target and press a button on the stick shift beside him. The coordinates were automatically fed into the TOW missile-launching system.

He held the scope in front of his right eye and quickly scanned the hillside. There was several detectable heat shapes in the viewer. Some were ambulatory. Men were moving on the hillside. But one heat source was unmistakable. The round barrel of a missile launcher shone in the scope like a tiny cherry Lifesaver.

Barrabas centered on it and thumbed the top button in the control. His hand moved down the shift to a trigger. A small red light inside the scope flashed.

The coordinates were in the TOW system. He squeezed.

The Huey shuddered briefly as the first TOW missile tore from the pod on the side. Two seconds later a fireball blew into brilliant existence on the side of the hill.

Barrabas had already sighted and set the coordinates of the second launcher. He fired again. A second fireball suddenly appeared, its close, compact flames illuminating the island.

"Take it up!" Barrabas shouted. The Red Vengeance still had at least two heat-sensitive missile launchers left, and if they didn't get out of range fast, one of those hot babies was going to find them.

Bishop adjusted the collective, and the Huey made a gut-wrenching swoop to gain higher altitude. He careened the chopper almost ninety degrees sideways and circled directly behind the fortress on the other side of the hill.

Barrabas sighed and sat back in the tiny instant between action. "Two down, two to go."

"We're going over the top, Colonel!" Bishop warned.

The long, winding peak of the hill was directly below them, and the top ramparts of the old stone fortress came into view again, with the lights of the little harbor stretching away below.

Barrabas searched the hillside through the FLIR scope again and sighted the heat residue of another launcher just as it fired. A big red splatter filled the scope.

"Three o'clock!" Barrabas shouted into the transmitter. He centered the FLIR on the heat source and set the coordinates again. Two BARB interceptors spun their green tracers from the Huey's fuselage.

The tracers vanished as another explosion erupted midair, directly over the fortress. Flaming debris fell like rain.

Barrabas looked down at the Red Vengeance headquarters. High stone ramparts were strung along the contours of the hill for several hundred meters. At each end they joined the natural barrier of the rock. Inside the ramparts the stone keep was built into the hillside. The windows of the keep were burning with light.

"We'll take care of that in a minute," he muttered. He squeezed the armament trigger. Again the Huey shuddered as another TOW tore from the pod.

"Go left along the hill," Barrabas instructed Bishop. He zeroed in on the fourth launcher as the loosed TOW struck pay dirt. For the third time a raging fireball blossomed on the hillside, its flickering flames illuminating the fortress from the other side.

Barrabas set the coordinates and unleashed another TOW. The last fire flower bloomed, and two smaller explosions kicked in as unused pirate ordnance blew up.

They had four TOW missiles left. And he could think of a use for every one of them.

"Where to first?" Bishop shouted.

"Let's cut off their escape," Barrabas told him. He pushed the FLIR scope momentarily aside. "The big trawler, floating out there in the bay."

The *Blood Maiden* was a kilometer away. Bishop made some slight adjustments to the controls.

"Hang on," the Canadian said, squeezing the throttle. The Huey seemed to sink momentarily, then the force of acceleration pushed Barrabas back in his seat. The chopper soared at a hundred and fifty klicks an hour toward the center of the pirate ship.

DREW WATCHED AS the great double doors at the end of the hall swung open and two men wheeled in a serving wagon of carved wood. The sides were draped with woven cloth, and a domed silver lid hid whatever lay on top.

The assembled pirate captains rose to their feet in a frenzy of shouts and cheers. The servant wheeled the tray to the head table where Ki Lim stood quietly waiting for it with a proud smile.

Their laughter and derision grew louder, and Drew put her hands over her ears to stop the noise. She sank to her knees as the cart was wheeled past. She remembered what Ki Lim had told her—Kyle would be there. She searched the room, baffled. There was no one present but the captains of the Red Vengeance and their underlings.

The raucous noise began to die, and Drew turned back to the head table. Ki Lim held his hand up to ask for complete silence. The servant had placed the serving trolley directly in front of the Great Leader, and he gesticulated toward it as he addressed the assembled captains. He spoke in an Asian tongue, leaving Drew ignorant of what was being said.

He finished, and his eyes caught Drew's. He smiled malevolently and spoke again to the assembled guests.

They laughed and looked at her.

Ki Lim reached for the great domed lid on the serving cart. He flicked his eyes at Drew once again and caught hers. She watched, hypnotized by the strange ritual. It was almost as if Ki Lim was taunting her.

Slowly Ki Lim raised the silver lid six inches above the cart. Then he tore it away.

The pirate captains cheered.

Drew blinked and shook her head.

It was her fiancé!

Kyle's head protruded from a hole in the top of the serving cart. He had been shaved, and wounded somehow, because a thin blood-edged line encircled his forehead.

The eyes in the immobilized head met hers.

He was alive!

Drew gave a silent prayer of thanks.

Kyle's eyes begged and pleaded for help.

She reached out involuntarily toward him.

Ki Lim's hand closed over Kyle's head. He looked directly at Drew and raised it. The top of Kyle's skull lifted neatly off like the lid of a bowl, revealing the glossy, heaving mass of his living brain.

Ki Lim began to laugh as the captains of the Red Vengeance cheered and raised their goblets.

Drew heard no sound. She saw Ki Lim's mouth open as he threw his head back in laughter. A loud roar of panic, ebbing and flowing like storm-tossed waves slapping the shore, tightened between her ears.

She looked at Kyle, unable to comprehend what she was seeing. His mouth was moving. He was trying to speak. She made herself listen, focusing her attention on his words. Slowly the roar in her head diminished, and the jeering sounds of the room filtered into her consciousness.

Ki Lim raised his hand again, signaling silence.

Drew's eyes were riveted on Kyle.

Ki Lim watched Drew.

Kyle's mouth opened. "Help me." His voice was a hoarse whisper. "Help m . . ."

Ki Lim's spoon swept down, plunging into Carrington's cranium and scooping up gray brain matter and blood. Kyle's voice cracked. His eyes whirred like the cherry wheels in a one-armed bandit. He quivered uncontrollably as if thousands of watts of electric current buzzed through his broken synapses. From far outside the fortress there was the sound of an explosion. Then another one, and in quick succession, two more.

Drew didn't hear them.

The world closed in on her, spinning darkness, and she sank to the cold stone floor.

BARRABAS TIGHTENED HIS FINGER on the TOW trigger. The Huey swooped down the hillside and over the water like a scythe. Orange muzzle flashes opened up on the *Blood Maiden*, and red-hot tracers slashed the darkness outside the windshield of the chopper.

Suddenly the Huey vibrated with hits. Barrabas sighted and squeezed the trigger, and the TOW shot from the side of the chopper, wagging a long orange tracer.

It was a direct hit just above the waterline. The *Blood Maiden* shuddered briefly. Seawater sizzled into steam against red-hot metal. Another explosion thudded through the ship. Orange flames burst up through the hull, blowing out the porthole windows level by level. The bridge erupted into the air, and the trawler was engulfed in flames.

The fire spread instantly as burning debris fell onto the decks of the fishing boats and trawlers anchored nearby. A solid sheet of flame burned across the water, and the little boats blew up like popping corn. "I love it," Barrabas said, grinning. "It's our ticket to everything. We've got three more TOWs to blow that pile of rocks off the hill."

Nanos shouted from the fuselage. "Hey, do we get a chance to shoot at anything or not?"

Barrabas leaned around. The mercs had their autorifles, grenade launchers and the M-60 primed and ready.

"I'll give you something to shoot at," Barrabas said slowly. "We're going to buzz the fortress. If you see something move, hit it."

Bishop veered the chopper in a wide circle until he was parallel to the walls that rose from the rocky slopes.

"Just a second now, Colonel, and I'll get in position for the TOWs." Bishop played with the rotor pedals, flying the Huey half sideways and angling the TOW pods on the left-hand side.

The walls loomed in front of them like a canyon of stone. Light from the inner courtyard outlined the defense works along the ramparts. It had been a grand old thing a few hundred years ago, but the electric lights were a giveaway and the walls were no obstacle. Not even for a flimsy beast like a Huey chopper.

The Canadian airman gained altitude until the chopper was high over the ramparts. The courtyard was bathed in bright lights, and armed pirates ran for the steps leading to the ramparts. Men on the walls went to their knees and raised their automatic rifles skyward.

"Got it," Bishop said. "We're going in like a pigeon shitting!"

The chopper flew straight and narrow down the long inner courtyard of the fortress, weapons protruding from all sides. Weapons storming. A hard rain fell.

Barrabas squeezed the trigger. The cross hairs in the sights met just above the doors of the keep. Almost instantaneously there was an explosion. The cloud of gray dust quickly obliterated a section of the courtyard. Flames licked up behind it.

Claude Hayes braced his legs. Recoil vibrations from the M-60 spread from his hands down his arms and shook his body. He gripped, moving the barrel slow and even as Nate fed the belt. The machine gun spat its long line of heavy death at the men running from the keep.

The bullets stopped them.

Flaming mummies stumbled out of the smoke and debris from the TOW. Some fell and burned. Others ran in circles, too hysterical to stop.

He knew what they wanted. Mercy.

On me, he thought. He tipped the barrel that way and gave it to them.

On the other side of the fuselage, Alex Nanos and Billy Two carefully aimed their M-79s, using defensive grenades for maximum antipersonnel effect. The shrapnel was deadly. The little launchers popped their contents like air bursting from a paper bag.

The pirates' prowess was at sea, not on land, against the undefended, not Nile Barrabas and the SOBs.

They grouped in pockets along the top of the walls as if numbers offered protection.

"Pick 'em out," said Alex, aiming the M-79. "And pick 'em off." He squeezed. Billy Two followed up with another. Lee handed both of them fresh launchers and moved into the middle of the door.

"My turn," she told them, elbowing in front. She leaned into Billy. The massive Osage was perfect support. She saw where she wanted to hit with one eye closed and fired the M-79 from the hip.

"Ouch!" The recoil stung her hand.

One by one their grenades burst along the ramparts. Small orange explosions flashed in sequence like light bulbs on a movie marquee. Men, bits of weapons and severed limbs tumbled over the sides.

The center of the compound was a smoking inferno. Barrabas saw a motor pool at the far end, and a dozen parked trucks, vans and jeeps made a tempting target. The survivors of the inferno from the first TOW blast were running for the vehicles. "Turn that way," he yelled at Bishop over the brutal noise of gunfire and explosions.

Bishop's hand moved on the cyclic, and the mercs rocked sideways as the chopper twisted. Barrabas squeezed the armament trigger as the chopper swung over the end of the compound.

The Huey bucked from the recoil, and Bishop yanked the collective hard. When the missile hit, the Huey bounced off the concussion, gaining altitude rapidly. The explosion hurled vehicular wreckage in a blizzard of metal shards. There was a sound like air passing through a gigantic diaphragm from the flash ignition of hundreds of gallons of gasoline. One by one gas tanks popped, adding geysers of liquid flame to the conflagration.

The Huey had gone past the fortress, and Bishop winged a sharp turn, heading back for a second run. "Last TOW, Colonel," he shouted.

Barrabas nodded. He was going to make it count. "I'll tell you when. We'll check out the resistance on this flyover, and if it's minimal, I want to go down."

Bishop lowered the front of the chopper. The Huey dropped like a seat on a ferris wheel into the maw of the burning fortress.

15

When the explosions began, Lac Sam was lying in her cell. She had fallen into a deep exhausted sleep, troubled by terrible dreams. In them she ran through stone corridors trying to escape unseen pursuers. But the corridors branched endlessly. There was no way out. Whoever was chasing her wanted to kill her, and she could barely stay ahead of them.

A loud boom, followed by a second one awakened her. The entire stone fortress seemed to tremble. She thought first of Drew, who had been taken away several hours earlier. She heard the distant thunder again and stood up. In its wake she heard rifle fire and other familiar sounds that she remembered from her childhood during the fall of Saigon. They were the sounds of war.

Almost immediately there was a deafening explosion that shook the fortress. The floor heaved and buckled, and Lac Sam fell to her feet. Blocks of stone fell from the ceiling and crashed around her.

She screamed and backed away, running for the door. The growing cloud of dust from falling masonry choked her. She screamed again for help and banged on the steel door. Another loud explosion shook the building, and more stones rained down, threatening to crush her.

"Please, please, let me out," she cried. In answer she heard keys jangling and the sound of the lock being turned. The door opened, and she rushed through it—into the arms of one of the pirates who had been guarding her cell.

His arm clenched her small body, and he chuckled lasciviously at her frightened, tear-stained face.

"No, no." Lac Sam struggled, kicking and pounding against him, trying to force him away. He struck her hard across the face and squeezed her to his chest. His hand moved to his pants.

The blow dazed her only enough to end her hysteria. The rapist had a knife in a sheath attached to his belt. She stopped struggling and reached for it. It slipped easily from the sheath.

She felt his hand sliding up her body. She gripped the handle of the dagger as tightly as she could, raised her arm and dug it into the small of his back.

The pirate stiffened as the blade cleaved his kidney. Lac Sam felt his foul, hot breath leave his body and his arms tighten around her. He fell, taking her with him.

For a moment she lay on the floor on top of the corpse. The dead pirate still held her, his grip frozen from renal shock. Lac Sam squirmed to loosen his hold. She pulled herself out of the deathly embrace, crawling over his head on her hands and knees.

She twisted around and sat on the floor. The fortress rumbled and shook from continued explosions and automatic weapons fire. But Lac Sam expected no rescuers. Whatever the pirates were doing, they were doing to one another. She thought of only one thing—escape—and not only for her. There were other Vietnamese women imprisoned there. And there was Drew.

The pirate's rifle lay on the floor near the body. She rose to her feet and picked it up. It was an unfamiliar type, but she recognized an automatic, and she knew how to shoot one. Every Vietnamese child knew how. If the Americans hadn't shown them, they had learned from the North Vietnamese.

Another explosion blasted the fortress. The electric lights flickered momentarily but held. Lac Sam ran down the corridor toward the stairs at the far end. She heard shouts and footsteps, raised the FAL and aimed it at the doorway. She fired when another guard came into view.

In her untrained hands the recoil from the three-round burst jerked the rifle upwards and to the right. It was a lucky break. A second guard came into view over the first guard's left shoulder. The automatic rounds stopped them both dead in their tracks. They looked slightly surprised and tumbled face forward down the remainder of the steps.

Lac Sam ran ahead and stripped the weapons from the guards. Bravely she slung them over her shoulder. Now she had three.

She took the steps two at a time. The other women, the ones whom the Great Leader gave away as favors to loyal pirates, were kept one level above her own cell. At the top of the stairs she heard male voices talking excitedly, then rapid footsteps coming down the corridor toward the steps. She pressed into the dark shadows in a corner. Two more men with rifles turned onto the stairs and began to descend. Lac Sam swallowed. She held the rifles behind her and called to them in a girlish voice.

The men stopped and turned in her direction. They could dimly make out the diminutive Vietnamese girl's outline. One of the men nudged the other with his elbow. Slow smiles spread across their faces. Their rifle hands relaxed, and they stepped toward the young girl easily confident of getting what they wanted.

Lac Sam pulled her own rifle from behind her, gritted her teeth and squeezed the trigger. The automatic sparked and 7.62 mm death slugged into their guts. The blasts knocked the two men off their feet, and they tipped backward down the steps.

Quickly Lac Sam darted back into the shadow.

From down the corridor another man called sharply for his friends. He was answered by the noise of battle outside the fortress. Lac Sam heard his keys jangle as he walked slowly toward the stairs. Then silence. She waited.

Nothing.

She gave up and stepped forward to strip the weapons from the bodies on the stairs just as the guard came around the corner. The thin tip of the FAL barrel struck the guard in the chest.

Reflex action.

She pulled the trigger.

The mag emptied bullets into the pirate's chest and out his back, the point-blank range impaling him on the tip of the barrel.

When the FAL stopped firing, Lac Sam let go. The pirate stood with the long automatic rifle extending from the bloody hole in his chest. His eyes were open, but he was dead. Then the weight of the rifle pulled him forward. Lac Sam jumped out of the way as the body fell.

She ran back to the wall and collected the two rifles she had left there. Quickly she stripped the three bodies on the stairs, abandoning the one with the empty mag. Now she had five rifles. She carried one and hoisted two over each shoulder. They were getting heavy.

Nearly staggering under the load, she peered around the corner into the corridor. Another explosion blasted the fortress. Stones fell from the ceiling, smashing lights set at intervals along the walls. She prayed to her ancestors to save a few lights, at least one, until she was out of the fortress and free.

Another sound rose above the din of battle. It was the wailing of women and their calls for help. Lac Sam ran down the corridor and under an arched door. The women's prison was in front of her, a long wall of bars cutting off a large, dark room filled with the imprisoned refugees. Flickering orange firelight came through the small, barred windows and danced on the stone walls.

The women, half naked or in rags, were packed against the bars, pounding them with their fists and shaking them in a mad effort to escape the embattled prison. When they saw Lac Sam, their arms reached through the bars as they pleaded to her for help.

Lac Sam ran for the cell and shucked the rifles off her shoulders. She unlocked the door and slid it open.

The enslaved women—twenty or thirty of them—pushed through into freedom.

"We have these." Lac Sam held up her rifle. "It is our only chance for freedom," she shouted.

No one had to tell them that.

They reached out for the guns.

"We will get more," Lac Sam yelled above the tumult, her voice ringing victoriously.

The women brandished the automatic rifles aloft and surged through the fortress, the inexorable waves of a rising tide.

THE CAPTAINS OF THE RED VENGEANCE rose angrily from their tables as the fortress shook from the explosions along the hillside.

One addressed Ki Lim. "We are under attack! Is this what you have planned to entertain us?"

"The woman with blue eyes has bewitched the Great Leader!" another shouted.

Ki Lim jumped over the table and walked into the center of the room to calm them.

"The attackers will be destroyed by the missiles. Have no fear," he assured them.

They looked at him doubtfully. Another blast against the hillside shook the fortress again. Chung Hee ran into the banquet room with another message. He looked white and frightened.

"Great Leader," he stammered. "We are lost!"

The captains of the Red Vengeance leaped to their feet, shouting angrily and demanding an explanation.

Chung Hee approached Ki Lim. "It is the helicopter as you expected. But the missiles did not work. They have destroyed the launchers and now..."

An enormous explosion beat against the fortress walls from the harbor. Ki Lim ran to the window. The *Blood Maiden* blew up in an inferno of flaming wreckage. The fire burned across the water on the spreading fuel slick, and the million-dollar trawler began to sink.

The little helicopter was circling at great speed around the bay and heading back to the fortress.

Ki Lim had been certain his missile defense would be a hundred percent effective. Doubt gnawed at him now. It was only the first taste of what he saw coming. Defeat.

"We have been betrayed!" one of the captains shouted. His accusation was met by a chorus of ayes. They backed away from the Great Leader.

Ki Lim turned from the window. "No! Stop! We shall defeat these attackers!" he cried.

"He is not our leader!" another captain shouted. The guests at the ritual banquet had turned into an angry mob. "The ritual was never finished. We are not bound."

Other captains of the Red Vengeance muttered angrily or cursed.

"We must finish!" Ki Lim shouted. The victim, Kyle Carrington, lay bound in the little cart near the head table, still very much alive.

"No!" someone shouted, louder than the rest of the noise. "We must defend ourselves!"

An angry chorus of assent answered. The assembled captains of the Red Vengeance turned on their heels and ran for the great double doors.

"Stop!" Ki Lim shouted, running into the mob of fleeing pirates, grabbing to hold them back. They pushed him away angrily and rushed from the hall.

BARRABAS FOUND JUST THE RIGHT SPOT for the Huey's last TOW. He sighted on a machine gun emplacement in a tower near the center of the compound. A moment later the tower disappeared into the atmosphere, machine gun, gunners and all. He nodded at Bishop to take it down.

In the fuselage Hayes and Beck mowed even lines of lead from the M-60 across the courtyard and over the ramparts. On the other side Lee Hatton, Billy Two and Nanos had dropped the M-79s and were using their automatic rifles.

The return fire had dropped to almost nothing, and dense smoke from the fires partly concealed the chopper. Bishop lowered the Huey with smooth, unfaltering precision, and the mercs exited before the skids touched down.

Their weapons blasted at a renewed onslaught from the frenzied pirates. A large number of hostile defenders started shooting from the ruined gates of the keep, withering them from a second side.

"Back to the Huey!" Barrabas shouted.

They retreated, and Bishop lifted the chopper slowly up, ready to pull out.

THE VIETNAMESE WOMEN who had the rifles were all experienced. Five of them marched abreast, with Lac Sam in the middle. They had learned well in the military youth cadres instituted by the government in their native country.

At the end of the corridor, where steps rose higher into the fortress, they surprised a group of guards who were hurriedly descending. The pirates saw a line of women. Then they saw a line of rifles.

They didn't see the muzzle flashes.

The women stripped the bodies, handing rifles, handguns and knives to the unarmed women. Together the armed force strode through the passages of the fortress, working toward the front of the building, dealing with the opposition as it went. No pirate who crossed its path lived. The cadre grew in strength until more than half the women were armed.

A monstrous explosion very nearby shook the stone halls and corridors of the fortress. Bricks and masonry fell from the ceilings, raining down on the women in clouds of choking dust.

Finally they broke into the long, wide corridor that faced the front of the building. High, narrow windows looked out on the compound, where a familiar type of helicopter was preparing to land.

At the far end of the corridor two great double doors were suddenly flung open, and dozens of pirates poured out. The captains of the Red Vengeance raced from the banquet hall, checking mags in automatic rifles and pistols, prepared to fight their way past the landing helicopter. Their leaders descended the staircase opposite the doors to the hall, waving their brethren onward.

Lac Sam and the others in the front line felt the women behind them pushing. A woman shouted, her voice dripping hatred, "He's the one who killed my baby!" She pointed to one of the escaping captains.

"And him," another woman said, singling out a second pirate, "he murdered my brother and sister."

The front line of women ran down the corridor, knelt and fired, dropping dozens of pirates. The second line fired over their heads.

The women who only had knives or iron bars pushed against the women in front. They wanted their chance, too. Finally they broke through and swarmed toward the pirate captains, screaming for vengeance.

Red vengeance.

Blood for blood.

Lac Sam quickly marshaled the women who had automatic rifles.

"Down the stairs! Let us get the ones who are escaping."

The corps of women split in two directions.

The pirate leaders reached the lower level of the fortress and burst out the main doors just as the Huey reached a hover a foot off the ground.

The chopper's machine gun poured withering firing from one side along the ramparts. The commandos poured out the other side.

The pirates edged against the walls, firing automatic bursts through the door, driving the mercs back to their chopper. Suddenly chips of stone and stray bullets winged past them. Some of the pirates dropped. The others looked around.

Some turned, raising their rifles to shoot behind them. A few threw their weapons aside and tried to run. Lac Sam and the women poured down the steps, cutting them down with single shots and three-round bursts.

"The helicopter!" one of the women shouted. "We must stop it, too!"

There were shouts of agreement. Several women ran to fire outside.

Lac Sam ran with the women along the wall toward the front door, unsure whether the helicopter was friend or foe. Just as they reached the doors, the commandos leaped from the chopper. She watched them emerge, one by one.

Two large men and a woman were followed by a man with white hair. As he raced to lead the group, Lac Sam saw his eyes. Glittering eyes of cold steel blue.

Lac Sam shivered. The commandos held grenades.

She turned to the women just as they went down on their knees and raised their guns.

"Stop!" she cried. "They are friends. They are Americans!"

DRIVEN BACK TO THE CHOPPER by the automatic weapon fire from inside the fortress doors, Barrabas considered his options. Bullets chunked at the metal body of the chopper. Bishop started to lift.

"Colonel, there's no more return fire from the ramparts," Claude Hayes told him. The machine gun was quiet. "We can turn the gun around...."

"We've got to get something inside there!" Barrabas said.

"Colonel, the enemy fire has stopped!" Lee shouted from the fuselage door.

"Bishop, take it down!" Barrabas ordered. "Let's go in there with autorifles and grenades."

Billy Two was first out, with Nanos and Hatton second. Barrabas jumped and ran through them, crouching in a zigzag run toward the doors. There was movement inside and glints of gunmetal like shiny slivers in the shadows. He tugged the grenade from his belt and raised the pin to his teeth.

Suddenly a young woman, half naked in torn black pajamas, ran from the building. She held an old Belgian FAL aloft and waved her other hand.

Barrabas's teeth tightened on the pin of the grenade. Was this trick or treat?

Other women came from inside the building, holding automatic rifles and handguns. They regarded the commandos with equal suspicion.

Barrabas heard the young girl in front shout, "They are Americans!"

Treat.

He ran to the young girl in front. She was small and delicately featured like most Vietnamese women. She had long black hair and blue eyes.

"Who are you?" he asked as he approached.

"My name Lac Sam. We are refugee prisoners here," she said, gesturing to the other women.

Barrabas quickly surveyed the ragtag group of young women, some of them almost naked, others dressed in tatters and rags. Their faces were dirty and covered with sweat, but their eyes blazed with the ruthless determination of victors.

"Are there more?"

"Inside are more. And more pirates, too." The other mercs caught up to them.

"Close your mouth, Alex," Billy Two muttered as he ran alongside Nanos. "You'll catch a stray bullet."

"Billy Two! Wake me up if I'm dreaming. Are they on our side or theirs?"

"Don't worry, Alex," Lee said, overhearing. "Women only fight for the good guys."

"All right, let's go inside and see what's left," Barrabas said, leading them through the throng of women, whose suspicion gave way to curiosity. The mercs glanced at the carnage inside only long enough to realize there was no life in it. Shots and then screams resounded from the upper level.

Barrabas raced up the stairs as women fled past him, panic-stricken. Their clothes and skin were red with blood, and they held knives. Bullets splayed the air and pounded several of the fleeing women in the back, killing them instantly.

At the top Barrabas threw his automatic rifle ahead of him and dived across the floor. A small Asian at the far end of a great hall fired the last of his

FN FAL's twenty-round mag. He held the long gun high and to the side at the end of its recoil.

Barrabas shot once.

The FAL caught the bullet and leaped from the man's hands.

Ki Lim jumped back, feeling the sting up through his arms. He looked for the gun. His hands were empty.

"No!" he cried angrily.

Barrabas jumped up. The front of his torso, his legs and his elbows were soggy with blood. It wasn't his. It came from the floor. The bodies of more than a dozen pirates had been hacked to pieces.

Ki Lim looked in the direction of the shot.

A tall man with white hair and blue eyes as hard as marbles glared at him and walked closer down the length of the room. His clothes were red from blood and his eyes spoke vengeance.

Barrabas kept his gun trained on the Asian as he slowly crossed the room.

"No," Ki Lim repeated. This time it was a whisper.

The SOBs pushed in the doors, and the other women surged behind them. Lac Sam ran to catch up to Barrabas. "He is leader of all pirates," she said. "He has killed many people."

Barrabas stopped short of Ki Lim and stared at him. The once-great leader shrank, pulling his arms in and hunching his shoulders. The thin mustache

TAKE 'EM NOW

FOLDING SUNGLASSES
FROM GOLD EAGLE

Mean up your act with these tough, street-smart shades. Practical, too, because they fold 3 times into a handy, zip-up polyurethane pouch that fits neatly into your pocket. Rugged metal frame. Scratch-resistant acrylic lenses. Best of all, they can be yours for only $6.99. MAIL ORDER TODAY.

Send your name, address, and zip code, along with a check or money order for just $6.99 + .75¢ for postage and handling (for a total of $7.74) payable to Gold Eagle Reader Service, a division of Worldwide Library. New York and Arizona residents please add applicable sales tax.

Remove from pouch...

unfold once...

Gold Eagle Reader Service
901 Fuhrmann Blvd.
P.O. Box 1325
Buffalo, N.Y. 14240-1325

unfold twice...

and they're ready to wear.

Offer not available in Canada.